Senatorial Revenge

By

Elmer L. "Corky" Snow III

authorHOUSE®

AuthorHouse™
1663 Liberty Drive
Bloomington, IN 47403
www.authorhouse.com
Phone: 1-800-839-8640

First published by AuthorHouse   3/24/2011

ISBN: 978-1-4567-5793-9 (e)
ISBN: 978-1-4567-5794-6 (dj)
ISBN: 978-1-4567-5795-3 (sc)

Library of Congress Control Number: 2011904566

Printed in the United States of America

To "My Mare," who brought happiness to life.

America's Tears are Painted Red, White, and Blue

By Elmer L. Snow

September 11, the world in a quandary.
We stood on the ground looking up into space.
Low planes a flying, families dying—
Could this be the end of the whole human race?

Tears were all falling, but this time was new;
Tears were now painted the red, white, and blue.
Innocence ending, America sending
A dish named revenge served cold just for you.

Doors had been opened to give you a try.
American eagle, Mom's apple pie;
Peace in our valley, food in our galley;
A cave in a rock pile is where you will die.

Some words to remember in case you've not heard:
America's mad, we won't mince our word.
We're ready each day for your best to test us,
But never the day that your test will best us.

So hear one America singing for you:
Catholic, Christian, Gay, and a Jew;
American Indian ready for war—
If this ain't enough, we'll give you some more.

One solemn voice, one final chorus.
Hear out the words we're singing for you.
Innocence ending, revenge we are sending.
Tears are now painted the red, white, and blue.

Chapter 1

Kirk Alexander's eyes were filled with tears as he watched, in childlike amazement, as the endless stream of uniformed police officers filed from their cruisers. He had never even imagined that there could be this many policemen in the whole world. Each of them walked from their cars in a long, solemn line. No smiles were visible in this gathering. They were tasked with the most unpleasant responsibility that anyone in law enforcement ever faces. Today, they would bury one of their own.

Kirk noted that each of the silver or gold badges had a small, black elastic band across the center of the shield. This was unusual for the child because he'd seen many badges in the past, but all were completely visible as the officer performed his or her duties. He instinctively realized this was one of their ways of paying their final respects to the body that had been gently placed into the coffin. The American flag fluttered slightly as the edges of the material were lifted by the slight breeze of the warm September morning. Kirk knew that the flag was one more sign of respect and honor for the deceased.

A shiver ran up the spine of the six-year-old as he realized that his father wasn't standing by his side, though he was with the hundreds of police officers in the gathering. Kirk's father, Detective Derrick K. Alexander Sr., would never again pay his personal respect to the body of a fallen comrade—because his was the body inside the coffin. A killer's bullet had ensured that Kirk and his dad would never stand side by side again.

The child looked up at his mother and suddenly gripped her hand tighter as the reality of life replaced the childlike fantasies that were designed for the young and innocent. Kirk would never see his daddy again, would never feel the roughness of his unshaven face when he returned from a day of arresting bad men, and would never again be able to run home from school to proudly display his artwork, which usually portrayed a police officer performing some aspect of his daily tasks.

As the youngster watched the sad faces that surrounded the flag-draped coffin, he noted the tears flowing from their eyes. There was consolation in the fact that his loss was being shared by others.

All in attendance suddenly stood at attention as three rifle shots echoed across the cemetery in rapid succession. As the sound of the final volley echoed, a lone figure away from the crowd began playing "Amazing Grace" on his bagpipe.

The chief of police ceremoniously accepted the folded American flag from the honor guard, sharply made an about-face, and marched slowly to Kirk's mother. Upon receiving the colors that had represented so much to the slain officer, Linda Alexander turned and knelt next to her only son.

"Daddy would have wanted you to have this," she said. As she wiped her eyes and then Kirk's cascading tears, she added, "He loved you so much and was so proud of you."

Kirk managed a weak smile for his mom. He knew that he needed to show her that he too could be strong in the face of loss and despair.

The police had buried one of their own. On that same day, a young boy vowed that his goal in life would be to keep others from experiencing the pain that he and his mother were living. Kirk experienced his childhood as a victim of domestic terrorism.

There would come a day when he would cease being a victim and would become a combatant in the war on international terrorism.

Chapter 2

Derrick Kirk Alexander Jr. had chosen not to follow in his father's profession, yet no one who'd known the father would deny that Kirk had certainly followed in his dad's footsteps. Throughout his life he'd maintained the highest level of integrity and had lived his young life as he thought his father would have wanted. After graduating from Bowie High School in Maryland, Kirk had accepted a scholarship, courtesy of the Prince George's County, Maryland Police Department, to American University in Washington DC. Despite the loss of his mother to cancer during his freshman year at AU, Kirk continued his course of study, where he would graduate with honors from the university with a bachelor's degree in political science.

While in his junior year at American University, Kirk's academic record, coupled with an outgoing, enthusiastic outlook on life, caught the attention of a philosophy professor, Dr. Robert F. Caldwell. After reading an assigned essay that Kirk had prepared on merits of revenge, Dr. Caldwell made a discreet call to an associate and previous counterpart in the Central Intelligence Agency. The call opened the door, and a lengthy, covert background investigation that would lead to the making of an employment offer that couldn't be refused.

Two months prior to his graduation, Kirk was approached by a recruiter from the CIA. Before the meeting was concluded, Kirk fully understood that he was being recruited as a covert operative who would serve at the pleasure, convenience, and direction of the US Government. He also realized that he would be joining the US Army upon graduating and could expect a minimum of three years of the most grueling training that the human body could endure.

Todd T. Lawrence, the agency recruiter, didn't mince words with new agents. "You'll go first to the army's basic training course at Fort Jackson, South Carolina. Upon graduating, you'll attend warrant officer's training at Fort Rucker, Alabama, where you'll be commissioned, upon satisfactory completion, as a WO one. From there, hold on to your ass, because you'll be doing nothing but training and learning month after month."

Todd Lawrence could have sold democracy to Stalin, Hitler, or anyone else who would spare ten minutes to listen. Throughout the remainder of his life, Kirk would say to select and trusted friends that following his recruitment, all he wanted to do was salute the flag and eat mom's apple pie.

Following their first meeting, Kirk's recruiter issued him a laptop computer and instructed that all significant communications would be sent to Kirk at an e-mail address. The laptop, upon signing on, would prompt the young agent through a series of computer firewalls that would establish complete security for exchanging messages with the handler.

"Your e-mail address will be Warren.Knicely@ExtremeMeasures. com," Lawrence stated in a matter of fact tone.

Kirk's face fell as he heard that name. "Todd, are you aware that's the name of the man who killed my father?" he asked in a shocked voice.

"Of course I am. His name will live longer than he will," the handler said. "Let's just say that retribution for killing a police detective, who was the father of one of our own, is beyond a wish—it's a given. The sun is setting on the life of Warren Knicely."

Todd Lawrence then proceeded to discuss Warren B. Knicely in-depth. Knicely was one of two sons of an itinerant farmer who drifted from farm to farm in southern Maryland, where he assisted in planting, cultivating, and picking crops. This was a farmer who wasn't a smart man, and there was only one subject he knew how to teach to his sons," Todd stated. "He was very adept in teaching hate to his kids—hate of blacks, hate of Jews, hate of anyone who represented authority, and hate of government. In fact, I've seen surveillance photograph's of Warren Knicely as he stood next to his father at the burning of a black church. He was around the age of twelve, crying tears of celebration and screaming the rhetoric that is usually attributable to their counterparts in the Deep South, who lived with the same attitudes.

"Eventually, Warren Knicely reached a plateau in life where he chose the churches to burn, one of which was located on the fringes of Prince George's County, Maryland," Lawrence added. "As I know you're aware, your father was killed while serving an arrest warrant for that church burning."

Todd went on to explain the role that Kirk would play if he accepted the employment offer. "Prior to September 11, 2001, radical groups of international and transnational terrorists, under the pretext of a jihad, were targeting Americans. Most of the attacks occurred in foreign countries, yet on a daily basis it was our own innocents that were being killed, injured, or kidnapped. After September 11, certain political powers decided that we'd had enough victimization. Now, we're taking a proactive approach to the worldwide problem that is using the United States as the battleground. In short, we're on the attack, and you will be one of the soldiers in this war."

For the first time in twenty years, Kirk felt that a tremendous pressure had been lifted from his soul. He knew that Warren Bryson Knicely was incarcerated in the Maryland House of Corrections and was serving a life sentence for the murder of his father. Instinctively, Kirk knew that Todd Lawrence had not only made a commitment, but he'd also given a solemn promise to see that an old debt was paid in full.

Kirk was also well aware that he was being afforded an opportunity to actually do something in the war on terrorism. It was a compelling employment offer in which he was being recruited to participate.

"Mister, you just hired yourself a new employee," Kirk stated.

Chapter 3

On May 23, 2003, Derrick Kirk Alexander Jr. graduated from American University with honors. As instructed by an e-mail he received during the evening of May 22, Kirk was to report at 0900 hours on May 24 to the US Army Recruiting Office at 1600 Jefferson Davis Highway, Alexandria, Virginia, where he should ask to meet with Staff Sergeant Hillyard. Kirk was not aware that the human resource offices for the Central Intelligence Agency were secreted in suite 500 of the same building. In a blitz of paperwork, Kirk soon stood with a small group of other volunteers and swore an oath of allegiance to the United States of America. Before sunset gave the final smile for the day, Derrick K. Alexander Jr. was a soldier in the US Army and was in a chartered van destined to Fort Jackson, South Carolina. Even the prodding finger of an army proctologist had failed to dampen the spirit of the young warrior, and he settled in the seat of the van and gazed at the neon lights of Alexandria as the bus proceeded south on Interstate 95.

Upon arrival at Fort Jackson and after being issued his military clothing and equipment, Kirk's platoon sergeant designated him as a squad leader. It was immediately pointed out that the benefits of this assignment meant having a private room and permission to maintain possession of a personal laptop computer, complete with Internet access. The signature of the CIA was written all over this position, although other recruits just felt it was a tool to ensure the squad leader could record every derogatory comment should he or she choose to destroy the career of another soldier.

For eight weeks Kirk diligently checked for messages on the Extreme Measures website. It wasn't until his final night before graduating from basic training that he received a message from Todd Lawrence.

"Congratulations on your accomplishment, and enjoy warrant officer training," the note read. "Please see the attached article from the *Washington Post*."

Kirk's heart began racing wildly as he read the attached article. The news report was headlined; "Police Killer Dies in Maryland House of Correction."

As Kirk read the article, he fully realized that a recruitment promise had been delivered in full. Warren Bryson Knicely, the killer of Kirk's father, had died just months before he was scheduled for a parole hearing. The newspaper reported that Knicely had died in his sleep from an apparent heart attack. The young soldier was fully aware that had he not accepted his employment offer, Knicely would probably still be counting the days until he could once again plague the citizenry of Maryland. "'God' is a three-letter word, and so is the CIA," thought Kirk.

The next afternoon, following a full dress parade outside Company A of the Sixth Battalion, Kirk boarded a bus with his military orders for warrant officer training.

Before nightfall, Kirk would arrive at Fort Rucker, Alabama, to commence his officer training.

Chapter 4

Chief Warrant Officer Kirk Alexander had been in a continuous training cycle for two years. He'd successfully graduated from the traditional training courses, and when nearing graduation day he would receive a message from Todd Lawrence, who would provide advanced notification—or in some cases, warning—of the next step. Kirk had most recently graduated from the Executive Protection Institute, a premier training academy in Berryville, Virginia, where he'd learned the techniques of bodyguard or executive protection work. From Berryville, he'd gone over the mountain to the Summit Point Race Course in West Virginia, where Bill Scott Racing (BSR) personnel had taught him the fundamentals of counterterrorist driving. The greatest aspect of his continual training was the fact that many of his training schools were operated by civilians and for the most part were attended by civilian security personnel from the corporate world.

With each school he attended, Kirk would pursue various search engines on his computer to attempt to ascertain the background of those who provided the training. He was convinced that Dr. K of the personal protection academy had strong links with many government and corporate heads. "Who would have thought I'd attend a bodyguard school to learn about etiquette?" he wondered. Such was the level of training that the agency was willing to provide for their employees.

Kirk thought he could see the writing on the wall when in June he received an e-mail that advised his next stop would be at the US Army Linguistics School in San Diego, California. Kirk had just completed six weeks of training at Fort Bragg, North Carolina, where he'd perfected the art of social extinction. He'd learned early on during this module that the course was designed to train one how to kill with only your own resources as the weapon. Alexander had proved his abilities through stealth and the talent of approaching a target from the rear and without more than a slight "pop." immediately and almost soundlessly breaking the neck of an adversary or target. "Not exactly what I want to put on a resume," thought Kirk. This ability did not go unnoticed by the cadre, and it was relayed to those who would have an intense interest in the proficiency of the young agent.

"Better learn to ride a frigging camel," thought Kirk when he found out upon his arrival in San Diego that he would be learning Arabic. His interest increased when he learned from a seasoned instructor at the training school that he would probably be taught "interrogational Arabic"—that meant he'd be trained to ask a question in the native language, then know what area of the balls to squeeze, or the fine art of waterboarding to ensure the truthful answer was forthcoming. Kirk didn't volunteer the information that he'd learned while training in the swamps of Okeechobee, Florida, how to use testicular investigative techniques, which was only one of many areas of the human body that could be useful in eliciting needed information in a timely manner.

Alexander had been given three days to settle in his new surroundings prior to commencement of his language school. His new home was a small, furnished apartment within walking distance of the educational facility. The residence was maintained solely for deep cover personnel who were assigned, for various reasons, to the large military complex of Oceanside, California. Kirk completely understood the concept that spending too much time in a group setting led to friendships, intimacy, and the sharing of life stories. In this regard, he knew he was an island, as completely separated from all other points of land as possible.

Of interest to Kirk was the fact that although he'd previously attended formal training in developing cover stories, prior to the language school, he'd never had instructions where he'd be living under his own name. Although he would use his own name, a completely revised life profile had been forwarded to him in the e-mails, which were also becoming less frequent.

Chapter 5

Nur Jasim watched her student as he walked up the sidewalk from the street. Her immediate perception was the casualness of his walk while he seemed to visually capture every detail of his surroundings. She guessed his age at twenty-seven (which was only a year off from the correct age of twenty-eight). At six feet one inch and two hundred muscular pounds, Kirk reflected a man who could fit into the most formal of situations but could also be depended on in the most critical of times. She carefully noted the closely cut black hair that spoke of a military barber. The young agent was dressed in a pair of beige Docker slacks with an off-white golf shirt. The fact that he was not wearing socks spoke of casualness in his philosophy toward life.

"Allah has sent the most tasteful clothing I've seen in a while and poured the most beautiful man he could have created into those clothes," she thought. Nur realized that visually this approaching soldier could pass as someone from the Middle East with the greatest of ease.

As Kirk entered the doorway of the office, he said, "I have an appointment with Ms. Nur Jasim."

"As-salaam alaykum. I'm Nur Jasim," she replied as she greeted Kirk in Arabic.

"Wa alaykum as-salaam," Kirk responded with a smile.

Nur was immediately impressed with the fact that her new student had at least done some preliminary research on his new language and had understood her greeting of peace. She would have been more impressed if she'd known that Kirk had seen the writing on the wall when he accepted his post–9-11 employment offer. He'd been self-teaching from myriad Arabic dictionaries and writings during his spare time for the last two years. Kirk knew the words, the context, and the sentence structures. He just needed someone to help him in his pronunciations.

The two discussed the contents of the course for the next two hours. Kirk was pleased to learn that his language instruction would be a one-on-one format and would not be solely confined to classroom teaching techniques.

"Because there aren't other students who might delay your progress, we'll take what you learn in our class, go outside, and use it in the world," she said.

Nur estimated that the course would last four months, depending on Kirk's ability to grasp the language. After seeing his instructor, Kirk would be perfectly content for this training session to continue for most of his career.

"Tell me about your background," the instructor said.

Kirk was ready with the answers. He'd spent three weeks of specialized training learning about the need for cover stories, how to fabricate them, what made them believable, and most important, how to provide the requested information without providing details that would contain any type of factual merit.

"I'm twenty-eight years old, a third-generation Floridian," he stated. "I was born in a small town named Ruskin, which is approximately twenty-five miles south of Tampa. I was a jock during high school and thought I'd have a career in sports until I arrived at the University of Florida and learned that my desire to play football surpassed my ability to play." Kirk paused and added, "It was at that point I just decided to settle for a degree in political science rather than a chance to move on to professional football." Kirk realized he'd said enough, and he knew that when one talked about not being able to fulfill a dream, it automatically threw a damper on the conversation, and it became a short lived talk.

After an hour of conversation, Nur knew absolutely everything and nothing about Kirk. "He's very talented in saying absolutely nothing," she thought.

Nur, on the other hand, was an extremely interesting lady. At twenty-eight she was the oldest of four children who'd been born in Zakho, Iraq. She'd been raised in the United States following her family's flight into Turkey from the Kurdish region of Iraq. She spoke frankly of the panic of living under Saddam Hussein and of losing many of her family members to the gas attacks that had been released by the cruel dictator. Throughout the conversation Kirk became aware of one thing: Nur Jasim

11

did not miss her former home and loved the United States. In fact, her proudest moment was the day that she and her family had received their naturalized citizenship while living in the state of Oregon. Kirk hung on every word that Nur said as she talked about her life and family. He would have been amazed to learn that Nur Jasim had attended almost all of the same classes Kirk had attended, and she was in her own right well versed on cover stories.

One item that wasn't open to any type of refute was her beauty. Her features were dark, almost to the point of a mulatto, with dark brown eyes and cold black hair. At slightly under 5'7" and weighing less than 130 pounds, she displayed an athletic body that would be instantly able to ascend the highest mountain or compete in a most grueling triathlon. Kirk could only imagine making love to this beautiful woman.

Within two weeks, Kirk and Nur were spending their mornings in their classroom environment and afternoons in the areas of Oceanside and San Diego. The instructor had a fast-track agenda, which was perfect for her student. As Kirk's grasp of Arabic increased, the teacher would move their class setting to whatever venue fit the particular language setting. When learning terminology that would be found around an airport, the two would go to San Diego International Airport to ensure the flavor of the words fit the content of the topic. Perhaps what he found most interesting was the fact that Nur was teaching him conversational Arabic instead of just the knowledge to interrogate or interview.

Within a month the two were conversing in Arabic with only rare exceptions, when Kirk would need to revert to English to identify a missing word or tense. Nur had instructed numerous students in Arabic but had never taught anyone who could grasp the language so readily. When sitting down for discussions, Kirk even gave the appearance of a Middle Eastern male and could easily pass for a native of her old country.

While discussing the Muslim religion, Kirk, although not showing any signs of conversion to the faith, seemed to quickly understand the background of the religion, and was able to discuss the stories of Islam with unfailing accuracy. Through the efforts of Nur, and dozens of books that addressed the Islamic faith, Kirk understood the religion as well as almost anyone who hadn't been born into the faith. Not only that, but Kirk had also learned so much about the faith that he could sit and argue the intricacies of the religion from any perspective.

The two sat on a bench looking out at the Pacific as the sun began to set in the west. "You know, I'm going to have to release you in a couple of days," Nur stated.

Kirk had known this moment was rapidly approaching, but he had held out some small glimmer of hope that it would be a topic that would come up later, rather than sooner. "I know," he replied. "I've been dreading those words for several weeks. You've taught me just about every phase of Arabic except the language of love."

Nur looked hesitantly into his eyes. "I'm releasing you on Monday," she said. "We have one last weekend to ensure every aspect of the language has been taught." As the two walked away from the view of the ocean, Nur squeezed Kirks hand. "I'm sorry to say that you'll have to learn the language of love through a correspondence course, or through another instructor." He couldn't recall when he'd been rejected with such class.

It would be Sunday evening before Kirk received his e-mail. The note from Todd Lawrence would indicate that he knew the agent was finished with his most recent training.

"You've completed your language course with excellent reviews. Report on Monday to the adjutant general's office at 0900 hours. You will discuss your pending assignment with Mr. Leonard Oathmeyer." A small map had been attached to the e-mail that showed the location of the AG's office at Camp Pendleton.

Chapter 6

At exactly 9:00 a.m. the following day, Kirk Alexander was shown to an office to meet with Leonard Oathmeyer. The only indicator of the position that Oathmeyer might chair was the fact that on the door to the office, a small sign designated the room as being assigned to Military Intelligence #4. As fate would have it, Lennie Oathmeyer was an operative who would, at least for the foreseeable future, replace Todd Lawrence as Kirk's handler.

"Kirk, I'm Lennie Oathmeyer," said the giant of a man who sat behind the desk. "It's been a long time."

Kirk studied the face of the somewhat youthful looking interviewer. "I'm sorry, but I don't recall our meeting," he replied.

"It was many years ago when I met you," stated Oathmeyer. "You would have been around six or seven at the time. I attended your father's funeral. At the time I was a young FBI agent working intelligence out of Washington headquarters. I eventually decided that the agency provided work that was more to my liking and abilities."

The young agent searched his memory with renewed interest. He immediately realized that he would not remember the face after so many years, especially because there had literally been hundreds of mourners at his dad's funeral. Kirk didn't apologize for not remembering because he knew that few people would remember the face after so many years.

"I was also sorry to hear of the passing of your mother," continued Oathmeyer. "She was a very nice lady." "Now, let's get down to our business."

Leonard Oathmeyer wasted no time in addressing his agenda. "As you know, Warren Knicely was taken out in the Maryland House of

14

Corrections. This was done as a favor to you and our country. We were the fate that intervened in his life. Just so you know, we'd originally planned on letting him get a release through a model inmate program, allow him to get comfortable on the streets, and then we were going to castrate the bastard before ripping out his heart," Lennie said. "We ultimately decided to accelerate the dying process in the interest of justice and to allow your own thoughts to be directed at something other than personal revenge."

Kirk was spellbound as he listened. "But I thought Knicely had a heart attack in his sleep," he asked innocently.

"Who in hell has a heart attack after waiting close to thirty years to ride the magic carpet called rehabilitated and released?" asked Lennie. "The bastard got his just reward, and we got our own reward—you. "We pride ourselves as a group that takes care of our own."

For the next two hours, Kirk listened in spellbound silence while Leonard Oathmeyer talked.

"For the past twenty- five years, our country has been led by total wussies," he said. "We've seen the intelligence function become a punch line in a living joke where the plot has been to do all you can for this great nation, and with luck you'll get shot, kidnapped, or bombed on a street corner by some jackass who doesn't know the difference in living right or equal rights. We finally have the leadership, both at the helm of government and right down to the lowest rung of the intelligence branch of a huge tree, and their mandate is to stop this madness.

"The powers that be have recognized that conventional approaches to solving the continuing problems are slowly and surely destroying our nation. This is where good American's such as you, I, and thousands of others who believe in America can start bringing peace and tranquility back to our society and security for our citizens."

Although a bit confused, Kirk was beginning to see the direction the conversation, or more appropriately the lecture, was going. A fleeting thought in Kirk's mind suggested that he start singing the Lee Greenwood song; "Proud to be an American." Leonard Oathmeyer was recruiting Kirk to be part of a small, elite hit team who would be responsible for terminating certain people and groups that were considered a threat to society.

"The Warren Knicely types will be removed from the population," said Oathmeyer. "They might serve their time in detention facilities, which have become training grounds for terrorist and recruitment centers for radicals, but it would be up to a few people such as you to ensure they don't waste much time in their trip from jail to hell. Although we may find it necessary to terminate some people in other areas of crime who are demonstrating destructive behavior, most of your work will be locating, isolating, and eliminating certain terrorist operatives who represent a threat to our entire country and her citizens."

Kirk had long ago decided that he was being hired to be a paid assassin. Now he realized that he was being recruited to be a soldier in a war against terror. Any reluctance in considering this aspect of his chosen profession had long since dissipated. There was one lingering question in his mind that represented a potential barrier for his own ethical concerns. "Would termination of a target be deemed necessary to inflict pain?" Kirk asked.

"No pain that isn't required," responded Lennie. "You do your mission as quickly and humanely as possible. We don't hire barbarians who enjoy their work. We just employ humans who understand the need for their chosen profession."

As Kirk listened and mentally reviewed what he'd been told, one issue was apparent. He was too far involved in the process to give even the slightest of thought to choosing another profession. He dismissed the fleeting thought with the justification that he would only be killing those who didn't deserve to walk among their intended victims.

"Mr.—uh, Lennie," Kirk said, "if I'm going to be working within the confines of the United States, what is the purpose of my learning Arabic?"

"Very simple," was the immediate response. "Our intelligence tells us that we have hundreds if not thousands of Arabic terrorists who are just waiting for the opportunity to commit another 9-11. Our employer feels it's time to close up the barn and start killing some of the livestock." Oathmeyer sounded casual as he said this. "Your language skills could become very beneficial to our team. Your training has revealed, uh, other proficiencies that will definitely be of assistance in reaching our goals. Don't just assume that you'll be spending all of your time in the states. This assignment will involve whatever international travel that's needed.

"Now, for your initial cover," Oathmeyer continued. "You're being hired by the Central Intelligence Agency, under the guise of the Federal Bureau of Prisons in Washington DC. We've determined that because our federal and state prisons have become such a lucrative recruiting ground for terrorists, it's wise to have personnel closer to those facilities and in a position that provides intelligence and information from a more strategic source. You'll fly out of San Diego at 0745 hours tomorrow and fly to

Dulles International near DC. A car and driver will be waiting at the luggage retrieval area, and you'll be taken to your new home. I want you to get settled in and report as instructed in this packet to your new job next Monday. You'll find a paper shredder in the office area of your new home. Ensure that you don't misplace this packet, and shred it when you have committed all the details to your memory.

"Call me at this number when you get to your residence in DC," said Oathmeyer. He then handed Kirk a manila folder and a business card.

Kirk almost fell out of his chair when he noted that the business card introduced Leonard Oathmeyer as the operations director for US Senator Royal T. Wingate, a Democrat, one of the most influential liberal senators who had ever been elected.

Chapter 7

The Honorable Senator, Royal Thomas Wingate had represented his constituency in the great State of Alabama for forty two years. Through his increasing influence—earned, gained, or stolen through his years of service—the senator had ensured that his candidacy was never challenged. Some opponents in the Capitol claimed that Wingate had gotten everything for Alabama with the exception of not having the federal government relocated to his beloved Mobile. The senator was so powerful that few people would dare oppose him publicly on the floor of the Senate. When one spoke maliciously about "Senator Royal," he or she did so in the presence of the most trusted ears and closed mouths. Who else but Wingate would call a sitting president on his private line and suggest the holder of the highest office in the land should start thinking more about the country than about interns. If you were an elected president of the United States, then you had felt the wrath of Senator Wingate at least once, and probably at least weekly during your term.

Although considered by many as the one elected official who would gladly give the United States to the poor, there was one area of Wingate's life that most had forgotten during his years of service. Royal T. Wingate was the son of a deputy sheriff who had been killed by a black man who was being sought for murder. Ironically, Wingate had been the same age of Kirk Alexander when his own father was killed.

Thanks to the mentoring, teaching, and philosophy of his own law enforcement parent, Wingate never attributed race to the killing of his father. "My father was killed by a criminal who just happened to be black," was the personal philosophy of Royal T. Wingate.

Throughout the years, the senator had acquired an inner philosophy toward criminals who preyed on their fellow citizens, and against terrorists who attacked anyone who failed to share their philosophy. "There are some among us who just don't deserve to see the sun rise tomorrow," Wingate often stated. His years of service to his constituents and his country had provided an excellent opportunity to glean supporters of this theory. There were some within the highest echelons of government who felt that Royal T. Wingate was a direct descendant of Attila the Hun but wore the clothing of a sheep to disguise himself.

A small wooden plaque on the senator's desk summed up his philosophy for government service: "Some people are destined to sleep with the dogs, but a faithful Democrat finds food for the people and the dog." In reality, Senator Wingate was about as close to being liberal as Attila was close to being a pacifist.

At seventy years of age, Royal T. Wingate was only too content to work late in his office, have a quick dinner at the fashionable Monaco Restaurant on Capitol Hill, and then walk two blocks to his ornate row house. Having been widowed for six years, R. T. had become used to an empty nest. The 5'10", 280-pound senior statesman took great pride in combing his fiery red hair in a swirl that sparsely covered a bald area that had been prominent since the senator's freshman year at the University of Alabama. In truth, Wingate bore a striking resemblance to an old and overweight Howdy Doody. The only difference was that Howdy was more handsome and definitely more likable.

Wingate's personal idol in life was Alex Trebek, whom the senator considered as one of mankind's smartest men in history. No one knew the secret that the senator wore Perry Ellis brand suits only because that was the brand that Trebek wore on his show. R. T. was so addicted to the Jeopardy show that he'd go through his house answering his own thoughts with questions such as, "Who is Royal Thomas Wingate, Alex?" There were some in the Washington inner circle who claimed that on the night that the senator's beloved wife died, he hesitated in calling an ambulance because he thought he knew the answer to final jeopardy and wanted to confirm his answer before addressing such a mundane subject as death.

Senator Wingate was the powerful chairman of the Senate Subcommittee on Criminal Justice of the Judiciary. In short, he ran the Federal Bureau of Prisons (BOP) by ensuring that the director of that agency had been handpicked by no one but himself. A short leash was all he needed to ensure his 140,000 inmates in ninety-five institutions throughout the country had access to drug abuse treatment, education, vocational programs, and life skills training. The senator could speak for hours on the successes of the BOP rehabilitation programs and how they had returned to the general population as productive citizens who never received even so much as a traffic ticket when they were released. Unknown to anyone except the senator and Leonard Oathmeyer, many of them didn't have an opportunity to break the law upon release because a certain team of overseers ensured they met with death as quickly as the ink on their release dried.

As chairman of his powerful subcommittee, Royal had ensured that he had his own staff to conduct internal surveys, investigations, and evaluations of ongoing programs within the Bureau of Prisons. Even the director of BOP, Polly Ann Gregory, was not privileged to information on this staff, even though they worked loosely under her stewardship. With a salary of $156,800 a year and a list of perks that would stretch from the Capitol to the Potomac, Ms. Gregory was only too happy to stay out of the senator's long reach.

Wingate knew that by having his team outside the complete control of the Central Intelligence Agency, he was protecting them from the myriad efforts that the enemy used to penetrate and identify members of the CIA. The Bureau of Prisons provided excellent cover, the same intelligence access as their big brothers and sisters in Langley, and kept the group away from prying eyes.

The senator had received the results of an in-depth study. When one identifies themselves as working for the Bureau of Prisons, the first question asked is, "How dangerous is your work"? When an employee responded that they were only involved in administrative affairs, no one had the interest to conduct further inquiries. An employee of the BOP was about as interesting as a termite exterminator who worked in the desert.

The exception to the rule was the fact that Polly Ann Gregory was one of the most sought after dinner guests on the Washington social circuit. She was known as witty and intelligent, maintained all of the required social graces expected of someone in her position, and yet had the most charming ability to invite an antagonist onto the street to settle an issue "man to man." Her success as a Washington insider was based solely on her ability to get the job done. The private line in Wingate's office was ringing as he walked from his private bathroom, drying his hands. He threw the crumpled paper towel toward the trash can, mildly irritated that he'd missed another shot.

"This is Senator Wingate," he answered in his distinct southern drawl.

"Sir," said Leonard Oathmeyer, "I've completed my assignment in California and am heading for the airport."

"How did it go?" asked the Senator.

"Great, sir; he's on board and should be reporting next Monday. I've got him flying in to Dulles tomorrow afternoon," Lennie added.

"Travel safe," replied the senator as he placed the receiver back on the cradle.

Chapter 8

Kirk's itinerary provided all necessary details. Besides a business class plane ticket, a completed employment application for the Federal Bureau of Prisons was enclosed that indicated the covert agent was applying for a position as a rehabilitation analyst for the BOP within their intelligence division. Alexander could only wonder at what legitimate aspects of the position he'd be required to perform. As Kirk reviewed the material, he noted a sealed envelope within the larger folder. Inside was an honorary discharge from the US Army. As Kirk reviewed the dossier he noted that there was no mention of any training school he'd been required to attend. This discharge only reflected that he'd attended basic training, advanced infantry training, and warrant officer school. In short, the man who'd done nothing but attend countless training schools to learn how to perform his craft was not recognized for much more than serving his country under honorable conditions.

"There should at least be enough in here to qualify me to join the American Legion," Kirk thought.

He had an urge to call Nur to see if she might be available for his final night in Oceanside. As he reviewed in his mind the thought of her enthusiasm and willingness to teach, he decided that calling her was an excellent alternative to spending his last night alone. Even though Nur had made her point in stating their business was just that, he did enjoy their conversations. A curt recording from "Ma Bell" in the local phone company advised that the number had been disconnected and there was no forwarding information. A somewhat puzzled Kirk Alexander packed his bags, cleaned his apartment, and set his alarm clock for 5:00 a.m.

Chapter 9

While Flight 2187 knifed through the thin air at thirty-five thousand feet, Kirk tired of reading and leaned back, closing his eyes and reviewing his recent life. He thought of the demolition training at Fort Ord, where he'd perfected the ability to fashion a crude bomb with nothing more than hardware store materials. His mind covered the map: his knife throwing training, where he'd perfected the art of hitting a three-inch area from twenty-two feet; his Arabic language training; a four-week stint inside a Hollywood studio where he'd learned to perfect a disguise in minutes. In between, there had been so many schools in his military career that he had trouble remembering some, but at the same time he knew that all of them might someday be useful in his assignments. He remembered with fright his own experience of being waterboarded in order to learn the effectiveness of that particular interrogational tool.

"Damn," thought Kirk. "I'm a spook for the Central Intelligence Agency." He dozed off and did not have another thought until the captain announced that the flight was on its final approach to Dulles.

Kirk immediately saw the sign that was prominently displayed by the limousine driver. His name was written on the cardboard that also advertised the car was from Elite Limousine Service. The agent wondered if this transportation franchise might be another agency front. His trained mind immediately told him that someone posing as a hired driver, in the right circumstances, might be able to fulfill an assignment without anyone taking more than a passing notice. He would file this thought in the arsenal of his memory.

As the car from Elite Limousine swiftly proceeded toward downtown Washington, Kirk carefully avoided getting into a conversation with "Joe," the driver. He merely rode along, enjoying the chance to once again be back in the area where he'd been born and raised. At least for the foreseeable future, Derrick Kirk Alexander was home.

Chapter 10

Although tired from his trip from San Diego, Kirk felt renewed energy as the familiar sites of Washington came into view. He was tempted to ask his driver what their destination was but then elected to enjoy the surprise of where he'd be living. The suspense proved to be rewarding as the limo pulled into the circular driveway of the infamous Watergate complex.

A door man was only too helpful in assisting Kirk with his luggage to the reception desk, where he learned that his apartment was on the twelfth floor of the historic building.

"Thanks to the Watergate burglars, there's a history associated with my new home," thought Kirk.

Within minutes he was registered, received two keys to his unit, and was riding the elevator to his new home. The receptionist, a beautiful young lady in her mid twenties, had given Kirk a welcoming packet that would contain all information he'd need to ensure every convenience that the Watergate offered would be instantly available to the new resident. He smiled as he rode the elevator to his assigned floor.

The apartment was spacious and comfortable, with every imaginable convenience a resident could ever want. Unknown to Kirk, there were several conveniences that weren't for his personal convenience. The CIA had immediate access to monitoring any phone calls that might be made from his room, a small video camera that was concealed in a smoke detector, and a computer terminal that, when used, would allow the tenants of a small office in the shadows of the Capitol the ability to monitor any messages that Kirk might send. There was one exception. A security firewall was in place to ensure that any e-mail messages that might be exchanged between Leonard Oathmeyer and Kirk would not be monitored by anyone.

Before Kirk unpacked his luggage, he made a call to Oathmeyer at his cellular number. After notifying his new boss that he was safely in his quarters, he was instructed to report to the Federal Bureau of Prisons the following Monday. The call was terminated after Kirk assured his employer that he had sufficient money to last for the foreseeable future. Kirk would have several days to shop, reacquaint himself with the DC area, and enjoy the fact that for the first time in several years, his only agenda was not to follow an agenda.

Chapter 11

As directed, Kirk arrived at the main building for the Federal Bureau of Prisons at 9:00 a.m. the following Monday. He'd had almost a week to acquire a completely new wardrobe and knew that he looked the part of any dedicated public servant who worked for the government. There was one slight deviation. Kirk had done his research through the powers of the Internet and had determined that Senator Royal Wingate was known to wear clothing that had been designed by Perry Ellis. Although he wasn't totally convinced that the senator was a knowing party to a small web of conspiracy, Kirk was aware that one never got a second chance to make that first impression. He'd opted to at least err on the side of discretion by carefully choosing the tailored navy blue suit, white dress shirt, and maroon tie. The young spy could have easily passed for one of the thousands of US attorneys who walked the streets of Washington without seemingly having a destination. In this case, Kirk knew exactly where he was going as he approached the security reception desk in the foyer of BOP, signed in, and was immediately directed to room 113 on the basement floor.

"I'm truly starting on the basement floor," thought Kirk as he rang the buzzer outside the door. There was a slight pause before the door was remotely opened.

"You must be Mr. Alexander," said the elderly receptionist as Kirk entered the office and approached another reception desk. "I'm Lois Harding, the administrative secretary for special investigations," she proudly added. "I'll be assisting you in processing in, and when we're finished I'll introduce you to some of our staff."

Any thoughts of what he could expect were quickly dispelled. Kirk found it hard to believe that contrary to finding a room filled with torture equipment, the area was like any government office that he'd been exposed to over the previous three years.

Lois led Kirk into a small private office, at which time she asked that he produce picture identification. Within minutes she'd reviewed the Maryland driver's license, reviewed his employment application (the same one that she'd completed just a few weeks earlier), and directed Kirk to date and sign the paperwork.

Although Lois Harding remained friendly and outgoing, it was obvious to Kirk that she wasted no time in accomplishing her tasks. Within fifteen minutes, Lois had taken passport photographs of Kirk and, after a short time in another office, had returned with cards that identified him as a "rehabilitation Analyst" for the Federal Bureau of Prisons.

"You'll be trained to process your own identity cards for the various assignments you'll be handling," Lois stated. She then went on to add that the office maintained a direct link with the offices of the US marshal's service, and when necessary, Kirk would be producing the same identification material that was used in the witness protection program to change identities.

"You'll become an expert on assigning identity and issuing your own passports, credit cards, driver's licenses, and any supporting data you require," she proudly added. "Now, all you need to do is take this card key, go back to the front door, and sign out. Then return to the security entrance on the south side of the building and enter the secured entrance that says 'Director's Entrance.'"

As Kirk retraced his steps to the first-floor entrance, he rightly assumed that his entry record at BOP would reflect an exit record, and he'd probably never utilize the main entrance of the building again.

When Kirk reentered the building through the director's entrance, he was aware that he'd just entered the same offices he'd previously been in, but through a private doorway. Lois was waiting as his card key opened the door.

"You've just had your only official contact with the BOP," she said. "From now on, it's the back entrance where there's no official documentation of your coming and going." Kirk nodded his understanding of the entry and exit procedures. "Mr. Oathmeyer is waiting for you," Lois stated as she led him toward a closed door.

Lennie Oathmeyer was seated behind a massive desk that could have easily been used by a sitting president while contemplating how to spread democracy to various corners of the universe.

"No calls, Lois," said the giant as she quietly closed the door to the office. "Have a seat, Kirk, and welcome to your new assignment. I'd wanted to be able to introduce you to our entire staff. All but one is on assignment; I'll have her meet you in a few minutes.

"This is going to be your first assignment," Oathmeyer stated as he handed a sealed folder to Kirk. "Your partner will work with you up to the point of final sanction. The two of you will work up the details and choose the manner, time, and location of termination; it will be up to you to close the case, so to speak."

Kirk refrained from opening the file and instinctively knew he should wait for the arrival of his co-worker. Oathmeyer continued.

"Kirk, there's one thing that needs to be well understood," Oathmeyer said. "You've passed the point of no return. In short, this is a job you only retire from; you never quit, never resign, never change allegiances midstream. Just so we both understand; you only leave our employ as a corpse or with a pension."

Although Alexander had intellectually known this information, but hearing it caused cold chills to run up his entire body.

"I'm at your disposal, with no reservations about my talent or reluctance to complete my tasks as directed," Kirk simply stated.

It was apparent this was the response Leonard Oathmeyer had wanted to hear. This was evidenced by the smile that crossed his face and the nod of agreement. "Well, let's see if she has arrived," he said as he picked up the intercom phone.

Within seconds there was a slight knock on the door. "Come in," Leonard stated.

The door opened, and Kirk looked up with curiosity and eagerness to meet his new associate. The look of curiosity quickly changed to shock as Kirk looked into the face of Nur Jasim as she walked through the door.

"Kirk, I believe you've met Nur under conditions other than her true role in our little network," Oathmeyer stated. "You can now forget her previous phone number," he added with a slight smile.

Nur smiled as she walked to Kirk and said, "I've looked forward to working with you in a more professional setting."

Kirk didn't miss the fact that Nur had emphasized the word "professional." He also didn't miss a beat when he stood, shook her hand, and stated, "I look forward to continuing to learn from you."

"Nur will continue her task of teaching you Arabic," Oathmeyer stated. "You're also going to find that she's very proficient in every assignment she's called on to perform. Now, it's time for you two to get busy. There's a three week deadline on your assignment."

Following the meeting with Leonard Oathmeyer, Nur led Kirk into an adjacent office where two desks were placed around a comfortable sitting area. Each desk displayed a keyboard and computer screen.

"That's your new work area," she said. "Perhaps it's time we became better acquainted," she said.

"My original assignment was to teach you Arabic," she stated. "Until last night I wasn't even aware that you and I were working for the same team. I know you can understand the confidentiality involved in the training aspect, and I want you to know that I'm thrilled that we're going to continue working together in this sordid life we chose."

This was an entirely new life cycle that would evolve into whatever direction the course of working together would take them. "It's kind of ironic," Kirk stated. "Once again, you're my teacher."

"Then let's get down to the business at hand," she replied in Arabic while opening the sealed folder.

Chapter 12

At the age of fifty-one, David Franklin Lowe had been incarcerated in the Colorado Federal Penal Institution for a month shy of thirty years. He'd been convicted as a young soldier for selling classified documents to a female Russian counterintelligence agent, who'd carefully sought out and subsequently recruited the young sergeant during his service at the Washington Navy Yard. An offer of friendship had led to a liaison between the recruiter and his target. The hook was firmly set in the summer of 1972 when Lowe became aware that his proclivities had been clandestinely recorded on film. Within days the soldier, in his haste to ensure his fraternization with an enemy agent wasn't disclosed, was making almost daily trips to the Lincoln Memorial, where he'd hand over top secret documents.

Unknown to Lowe, the Federal Bureau of Investigation already had more than a passing interest in the foreign agent. Their surveillance of her almost immediately led to the identification and surveillance of Lowe.

Although his arrest was almost immediate, Lowe had disclosed enough information that ensured two deep cover agents working in Pakistan had been killed. The Russian envoy, Natasha Milenticoff, had been sent out of the United States along with her diplomatic immunity status. Lowe had been sentenced to thirty years at hard labor in Colorado.

Lowe hadn't even bothered with appearing at several parole hearings he'd been scheduled for during the past five years. He knew the interviews and begging would have fallen on deaf ears, and he chose to maintain the self-respect he'd earned throughout his life of incarceration by not asking anyone for favors. He only had days left of his sentence and knew that through the assistance of Melanie McCall of the Bureau of Prisons outreach program, he stood an excellent chance of getting a good job in the town of his choosing. He'd also seen the way Melanie looked at him and was convinced that she was willing to share more than employment assistance.

"He knows me as Melanie McCall," Nur told Kirk. "I've visited him on numerous occasions, and he's placed enough faith in me to hint that with a new identity he could completely walk away from the past. Would you believe that he intimated that there might be a better future for me if I hung out with him for a while?"

Kirk couldn't resist saying what crossed his mind. "Maybe I'd be better off just killing you rather than a different boyfriend every week."

Nur first gave an incredulous look at Kirk and then began laughing hysterically. The private joke was an obvious indication that the agents would enjoy working as partners.

The couple worked for several hours in a review of Lowe's file. They identified all family members who still maintained contact with the prisoner and were soon obtaining phone listings on every number he'd called during his period of incarceration. One listing was to a personal advertisement column in a Colorado newspaper.

"I can't believe that prisoners have this much freedom," Kirk stated.

Nur had accessed the newspaper and, upon entering a few key words, was led to a website through her computer.

"This has to be him," Nur said. The personal ad had been written two years previously and informed the reading public that an inmate in the local penitentiary would be released in a short time, and the author was willing to share his thirty-year supply of seminal fluid.

Nur immediately printed out the personal note and turned to the file.

"Here it is," she stated. "Two years ago, Lowe began receiving mail from Delores Holcomb, 224 Venice Street, Colorado Springs, Colorado. Since then, he's received at least two letters a week from her."

Kirk was beginning to see the logic of the exercise. David Lowe had created his own paper trail that would enable the assassins to track him down upon his release.

"It appears that Delores might have been able to promise more than you," Kirk stated, and then he jokingly added, "But remember, it's better to have loved and lost than wake up for a 2:00 a.m. feeding."

"I could just kill him for cheating on me," Nur replied.

The humor was not lost on either of the two as they continued to review the file and began planning their task.

Chapter 13

Nur sat waiting in the interview office at the house of correction. Since this would ostensibly be the last time she would interview Lowe, she had chosen just the right clothes to ensure he knew there was life outside the century-old penitentiary.

"I've missed talking to you," David stated as he was led to the room and allowed to enter alone. As usual, a guard would remain outside the door but wouldn't be privy to the conversations between the prisoner and his counselor.

"I wanted to come last week, but my office insisted I tie up some loose ends on a client I was helping in San Francisco," she replied.

Lowe sat across from Melanie and immediately let his eyes explore the miniskirt she wore. Melanie deliberately bent over to retrieve a pen from her purse, exposing more cleavage than he'd ever seen on the woman who was going to help him find his niche in society. Three decades of abstinence slammed inside his testicles as he realized that in two days he'd finally have his choice of women in the world.

Nur pointed to a card on the table and said, "This is the name and number of an old friend of mine who has a talent for hiring good people who want to earn a lot of money." The card bore the name of Claude Stocksdale and provided a Denver exchange telephone number. "Don't call Claude until Wednesday," she stated. "He's in Houston until then."

Lowe wasn't aware that the card had been emptied from an envelope prior to his entering the room and therefore didn't realize there were no fingerprints on the card. The convicted spy retrieved the card, viewed it, and then placed it into the pocket of his denim shirt.

"I wanted to see you tomorrow when you're released, but I'm not going to be back at my motel until around 5:00 p.m.," Nur added.

"Where are you staying?" Lowe immediately asked.

"I have one of the government discount rooms in the DeLeon Plaza on Route 16," she replied. "Then I fly out the following morning."

Nur knew the question was coming when she slightly shifted her legs in a manner that would rival Sharon Stone from her famous scene.

"Can I come by and perhaps buy you dinner?" asked Lowe.

Nur breathed a sudden deep breath that sent the message that she was tempted to taste the forbidden fruit. "Oh, if I were caught …," she began.

"No one will ever know," Dave pushed. "I just want the opportunity to talk with you about life, what to expect, and more about this new job."

"Make it at 6:30 p.m.," Nur quickly stated. "And, for God's sake, keep this between us because my job is on the line. I'm in room twelve, so don't ask at the office but meet me at my room." She gave one last visible view of most of her inner thigh as she stood up to leave.

"You're worth every bit of the past thirty years," he stated. "I'll be there!"

As Nur walked from the front entrance of the Colorado Federal Penitentiary, she dialed a pre-programmed number on her cellular phone. "Mission accomplished," she stated.

"I'll see you at the hotel," replied Kirk.

Chapter 14

Nur and Kirk had been in Colorado for three days. They had conducted their due diligence and had their plan in place. The two had located the DeLeon Plaza, which offered a vantage point of being away from the busy area in a more remote location. There were no surveillance cameras on the premises that could seal one's fate by capturing images on video, and there was a liquor store approximately a mile south of the motel on Route 16. Although the exterior of the motel was respectable, its location ensured that most patrons would be residents by the hour, and cash would be the motivator in obtaining a room.

Nur knew that prisoners were released at exactly 12:04 p.m., minutes after the noonday whistle at the penitentiary. This would mean that David Lowe would walk into the welcoming arms of freedom within minutes of that time. A prison van would take the released prisoner to the bus terminal in Denver where there would be the customary wish of good luck—and a new problem would then vanish into society.

While Nur, posing as Melanie McCall, had been baiting the prisoner, Kirk was carefully conducting additional surveillance of the entire area. When satisfied that there was nothing further he could do until the following day, when Lowe was discharged, he returned to the Hilton to wait for the return of his partner.

When Nur returned to the hotel, she again called him on his cellular phone. The two agreed that it would be safe to meet in the lobby bar to further discuss their elaborate plan.

Chapter 15

At exactly 12:08 p.m. the following day, David Lowe walked from the front entrance of his home for the past thirty years. He was a free man ready to earn money and fantasizing about the treat he would have that very evening. He walked to the older model Ford window van that was property of the State of Colorado and that would transport him into Denver.

At 2:43 p.m., Lowe climbed from the van in front of the bus terminal. With a small suitcase in his left hand, he quickly shook hands with the driver and disappeared into the station.

As anticipated by Nur and Kirk, Lowe walked immediately to a pay phone, retrieved a card from his wallet, and dialed the phone number of Claude Stockdale. There was no response other than a phone recording that stated that Stockdale would be out of town until the following day. A caller ID recorded the calling number.

Lowe's second call had also been anticipated. He called his pen pal, Delores, and informed her that due to some red tape, he wouldn't be released until the following day. They agreed that she would meet him at the bus station the following day at 2:45 p.m. The paroled prisoner had only two items left to do: enjoy a few drinks and take a cab to the DeLeon Plaza.

As Lowe walked from the bus station into a bar that was located two blocks from the terminal, a lone figure watched as he entered. Kirk returned two blocks to the bus station, where he purchased a small black suitcase, similar to the one carried by Lowe. The male then grabbed a cab and instructed the driver to take him to the DeLeon Motel.

There was no conversation as the yellow cab proceeded to the motel.

The passenger for the ride, exited the cab, and entered the motel office. As requested, room twelve was available, and the clerk hoped "Mr. Lowe" enjoyed his stay.

Kirk used a handkerchief to turn the door knob as he entered the bleak room. He grimly noted that the size of the room would roughly be the equivalent to a jail cell. Upon gaining entry to his room, Kirk reached inside his pocket and retrieved two surgical latex gloves and carefully put them on his hands. He then removed a knit cap from his pocket and placed it on his head. Kirk did not want a loose hair to fall anyplace in the pending crime scene.

He turned on the television and watched CNN while he waited for his quarry.

Nur Jasim, wearing a blonde wig, sat in her rental car approximately 150 feet from the entrance of the bar that David Lowe had entered. At exactly 6:00 p.m. he walked from the bar carrying his small valise. After standing in front for several minutes, Lowe hailed a cab.

Nur conducted a loose tail until she was certain the cab was heading toward the DeLeon Motel. At that time, she removed her cellular phone from her purse and dialed Kirk's number. She let the phone ring once and then hung up.

The trap was set, and the animal was on the way to the slaughtering pen. Nur could faintly see the cab as the driver negotiated onto the highway where she and Kirk had conducted their advance work.

Kirk waited patiently. He decided to change television channels to a game show that could be just loud enough to be heard from outside the door.

He heard the sound of a car outside of room twelve. There was a pause, obviously while Lowe was paying his fare, and then he slammed the car door. Kirk heard the taxi drive away and waited for the knock on the door.

It was a slight, timid knock. Kirk quickly looked around the room and then opened the door, ensuring he stood behind it to conceal his view. David Lowe walked into the room, and while turning to face his hostess, whom he'd dreamed of for several months, he opened his eyes in surprise and then shock. Kirk's hands were outstretched as he grabbed Lowe by the neck and pulled him completely into the room while closing the door with his own body. There was no resistance from David as his neck snapped and life drained from his body. Thirty years of seminal fluid as well as the morning's breakfast were emptied into the trousers of the prison-issue suit as the turncoat American met his maker.

Kirk allowed the body to fall just away from the doorway to ensure he had ample room to exit. He risked a quick glimpse from the drawn curtains and then picked up his valise and walked from the room. A gray Ford Taurus was parked just north of the doorway. As Kirk entered the passenger side door, the vehicle casually drove from the parking lot, leaving the flashing neon lights of the DeLeon blinking excitedly in the rearview mirror.

The two assassins would be in Washington DC before the body would be found. Despite the best efforts of the Denver Police Homicide Squad, their investigative efforts would hit a brick wall when they determined that a card in the victim's wallet in the name of Claude Stockdale was their only lead. As fate would have it, Stockdale had himself been convicted of selling secrets to the Russians in years past.

Lieutenant Damon Scott perhaps summed it up best when he advised his lead homicide investigator to close the case inactive. "Hey, the damned Russians waited thirty years to commit revenge. They were behind it, and we can't convict Stockdale, so let's just make the rest of his life miserable." Even the Denver police had their own sentiments toward those who would sell national secrets to the enemy.

Leonard Oathmeyer was pleased with the performance of his two commandoes.

Chapter 16

Kirk spent the better part of his return flight to Washington going over the details of his first assignment. Surprisingly there was no regrets resultant from taking his first life. In fact, Kirk felt a deep sense of satisfaction in the way that he and Nur had worked together. He carefully and methodically replayed his mental video of the entire sequence of events and was unable to identify any frame that would point a finger of guilt or suspicion in his direction.

As Kirk and Nur took their return trip to Dulles Airport, Leonard Oathmeyer sat in a small, soundproofed room with Senator Wingate.

"I'm extremely pleased with the way our two employees worked this assignment," Lennie stated. "I've meticulously gone over their plans and found nothing but a professional result."

The senator agreed. "I think you used good judgment in starting them on something a bit simple but that needed to be done. And we know that our source in Denver will keep the investigation from taking any "testosteronic" attempts from some young detective to make a name for himself in solving the killing of a spy."

Both Oathmeyer, and the senator were convinced that this particular continuation of training was necessary. Personnel were started on a simple assignment to ensure they would gain the expertise to handle the impossible ones.

What Kirk and Nur were not aware of was the fact that while they were taking the life of David Lowe, a lone figure maintained continual surveillance on the operation to ensure that if the covert assassins failed to complete their mission, the operative would complete the assignment as well as ensure that Kirk and Nur would be terminated to ensure their silence. The spy business was based on the premise "Trust, but verify."

Chapter 17

Nur and Kirk were in their office at the Bureau of Prisons early the following Monday. Although they hadn't had contact since leaving Denver, the two were anxious to discuss their first assignment together and devise ways that would ensure future details were dispatched as efficiently.

"First," said Nur, "let's destroy our identity from Denver."

The duo meticulously went through their wallets and removed the credit cards, driver licenses, and any documentation under the assumed names they'd used in Denver. They carefully placed them in a document shredder that effectively erased the identity of Claude F. Gilpin and Melanie McCall, the aliases under which the twosome had traveled.

"You'll find in this business that you'll need a phone book to keep up with the supply and demand of our jobs," Nur said with a smile.

Kirk nodded his reply as he fed the last business card of Claude Gilpin, an IBM sales consultant, into the shredder.

The agents had completed their tasks well before their scheduled 10:00 a.m. meeting with Oathmeyer.

"Well done," said Lennie Oathmeyer as the covert operatives sat down with their handler. There would be no further comments on the success of the Denver sanction. There would be no need for further discussion because Oathmeyer had received a detailed report from his trusted deep undercover operative who'd been surreptitiously present during the completion of the mission.

"On May 10, 1998, Masoud Ali Al-Wakim went into the restaurant of the Cairo Hilton while carrying a somewhat aged leather briefcase," Lennie stated. "He ate a leisurely breakfast of fruit, drank a large orange juice, paid his bill, and left—without his briefcase. Within ten minutes of his departure, the briefcase exploded, along with two pounds of plastique. There were ten fatalities, including the four family members of the Davis clan from Chicago. Sidney, Allison, Franklin, and Melissa were visiting Cairo as a present to Melissa, who'd just graduated from Ohio State with a degree in Egyptian studies.

"There are some concerned elected officials who feel that it's time that Al-Wakim pays for his senseless killing of an American family," Oathmeyer solemnly stated. As he handed a thick folder to his two assassins, he added a simple directive. "Make sure this man knows why he's been selected. Tell him that the president of the United States of America sends his regards," Lennie added.

The two operatives returned to their work area without further conversation.

Chapter 18

As Nur and Kirk read through the thick file, they realized the extent of the investigation that had been conducted through various agencies—including Central Intelligence, Military Intelligence, members of National Security—and through hundreds of interviews, interrogations, informant bribes, and surveillance.

Masoud Ali Al-Wakim was fifty-four years old. For the past seven years he'd lived in Paris, France, where he actively served as a contact intermediary between several suspected and known terrorists. Masoud was a Sunni Muslim who'd been born in Iran, where he'd received his education that included an intense hatred of all nonMuslims; he had an advanced degree in hating Americans. Perhaps the only redeeming quality about Masoud was his propensity to take several baths a day.

Kirk wondered how some of the facts had been obtained because they were so thorough in their content.

The terrorist had been located during a satellite monitoring of a suspicious cellular call from an Al Qaeda terrorist that subsequently brought intelligence gatherers to within ten feet of the front door of Masoud's modest apartment in Paris. Surveillance and photographs had served the intelligence community well.

After reading and re-reading the file, Nur and Kirk both realized they would appreciate the opportunity of pointing their killer in a direction toward a firsthand visit to Allah.

The two worked well through the day as they conducted the preliminaries on their pending trip to Paris.

Their first priority was to establish a new identity for their trip to France. After a quick consultation with Lennie, it was determined that the agents would travel as husband and wife. Although Lennie didn't like for his operatives to bunk together, he recognized that a husband and wife on business travel would be easier in preparing the logistical aspect of the trip.

Nur and Kirk selected the names of Jeffrey and Cherise Lonigan, compliments of the Richmond, Virginia, phone directory. From there, they established their cover stories that would work in their planned travel. The Internet provided an occupation for Jeffrey. In two weeks, hundreds of representatives of the International Press and Media Association would be gathering for their annual convention in Paris. Jeffrey C. Lonigan, a writer from the Richmond Tribune, would now be attending.

Through their endless computer data bases, the two prepared the necessary papers, including an official exact copy of press credentials that was instantly issued by the International Press and Media Association through the complements of a BOP database system.

By midafternoon, Nur had registered the couple at the posh Le Marquis Hotel at 14 Rue Dupleix in Paris. "I chose this hotel because they have in-house entertainment," Nur stated with a slight smile. Their American passports reflected they'd been issued four years previously and showed the wear and tear of four years of occasional usage in travel to Germany, France, and a two-week sojourn to Greece, where Jeffrey had been sent for his job. Jeffrey's passport showed more wear and tear, which was consistent with travel of a reporter who went to the story rather than waiting for it to come to him.

A review of a map of Paris had revealed the hotel was just a few blocks from 110 Rue de la Roquette, which happened to be the residence of Al-Wakim.

While engrossed in the minutia of their planned travel, Nur contacted the airline and used her ten-minute-old credit card to make reservations for the couple on Flight 2027, which would depart Dulles Airport on April 4, 2006. The return flight was left open because Mrs. Lonigan was unsure if her husband would be meeting with the executive committee following the conference.

Upon completing the flight arrangements, she immediately went to another database that printed a "used" ticket that indicated the pair had flown from Richmond to Washington on April 3. This receipt would be maintained with the passport and other tickets to ensure an alert customs official would be able to verify that their travel had originated in the city of their residency.

As the spies worked together, Nur would recite what she'd done and provide the logic behind her activities. Kirk was truly furthering his own education and future expertise by watching his methodical partner as she prepared their itinerary.

It was Kirk who suggested the need for wedding rings for the married couple. "Great suggestion," Nur replied as she quickly walked to another room, opened a filing cabinet, and removed a man's gold wedding band. She opted to use a more modest diamond ring for herself rather than take "Big Bertha," which was available for the most extravagant of undercover functions. Big Bertha was a three-carat solitaire diamond that was laughingly referred to around the office as the mother of all marriages.

They both worked through the day and continued for the next two days, preparing for their trip. Because they had another week and a half before their planned departure, the two spent hours memorizing the most recent satellite maps of the city of Paris. Through the use of a virtual reality computer program, the operatives spent countless hours wearing a small headset with optical lenses, during which they could sit at their desks in the city of Washington and make the complete journey from their Paris hotel, walk North on Rue Depleix, travel two blocks to Square de la Rogette, and with complete detail, proceed to the home of their terrorist. Virtual reality had the capability of showing every detail of the neighborhood, including the homes, people, passing cars, traffic lights, and sidewalk cafés that were in the area. The program was so detailed that after Nur and Kirk knew every detail of their travel through the areas they would be conducting their assignment. Problems were also programmed into the situation; the operators could make an armed French police officer suddenly appear, and it would then become necessary to utilize alternate routes through alleys or certain restaurants or shopping stores that had the availability of exiting through back doors or fire exits.

"It's a great way of avoidance without confrontation, and escape as opposed to capture," stated Nur.

To Kirk, it was an opportunity to play the world's most exciting video game and to learn, through trial and error, how to win. He had an almost boylike enthusiasm for the planning as he tested himself at increasingly difficult levels. Suddenly he would bring more police officers into the program, then members of the military, as they chased him through the streets of Paris. Only once, while escaping through an alley that he'd traveled in dozens of fictional trips, did reality hit home. A Middle Eastern male appeared from behind a trash dumpster and pointed a gun directly at

Kirk. The program stopped at that moment, a clear message to Kirk that he'd lost his life.

"Reality can make a person humble," he thought.

On Thursday, Lennie brought a video tape into their office and handed it to Kirk.

"I want you both to review this until you can't stand watching it anymore," he stated. "Then, watch it again."

According to the dates on the video, it had been taken the previous morning. The video, complete with times and date, showed a car pulling into the front of Masoud's residence, parking in front of the door, and a giant of a man getting out and walking around behind the vehicle, where he opened the right rear passenger door after looking completely around the area. As the car door opened, Al-Wakim immediately got out of the car and walked six steps to the front entrance, which was promptly opened from inside. When the terrorist entered the door of his residence, the driver—or more appropriately, his bodyguard—returned to the car and drove approximately twenty yards into an open garage. The bodyguard returned to the residence, opened the door, and went inside Al-Wakim's residence. The video ended.

"What do you think, Kirk?" Nur asked.

"There's a couple of weaknesses," he replied. "If we were waiting around the doorway, the driver would obviously select safety alternatives and keep driving. And, someone inside is apparently alerted so that they can unlock the door and open it when the car stops."

Kirk focused on his memory of the video and added, "The person inside the home is leaving the door unlocked so that when the driver parks the car and returns to the house, he can enter without using a key. We have an option of getting into the home during that time span when the driver is entering the garage, parking the car, and returning to the house. But we'd have to take the driver out when he enters the home. We don't know how many people are inside the home in addition to our target, and we have no idea of the interior of the home. I see it as a real dilemma."

After reviewing the video, Nur shared her own interpretation of the issues. "I could take the driver out as he starts to exit his vehicle after parking it. That way, your back will be covered. You, on the other hand, could use the exact moment that the driver pulls into the garage to enter the house. You'll be out of his view, enter the house, and take out the bad guys."

The assassins ultimately decided that the unknowns were greater than the known. In short, the risks were increased when the future was unknown. The two would have to reduce the threat to them to a more acceptable level.

The value of the recent video was immeasurable. The two had pictures of Al-Wakim that were actually only hours old. They were able to distinguish his walking characteristics, style of dress, and physical appearance.

When the couple shared their thoughts with Lennie, he agreed with the logic of their reasoning. "We'll attempt to obtain additional video before you depart," he stated. "Incidentally, wear old clothes to work on Monday. I have you both scheduled for some refresher training."

Chapter 19

Lennie Oathmeyer was the only business contact that Leslie McCarter maintained in the US government. Leslie, more appropriately known as The Broom, had the task of sweeping potential problems under the rug when an operative might fail in their mission. The Broom lived in a small efficiency apartment in Crystal City, Virginia, just minutes from the Ronald Reagan Airport.

At sixty-four years of age, The Broom looked every bit his age. At 5'10" and 185 pounds, his rugged face and graying hair belied a man who'd had more than a hard life. He was a man who was well liked by his neighbors, who just knew him as a retired postal carrier who could have been every child's favorite grandfather. Neighbors were more than impressed that by his living a simple and modest lifestyle, Leslie was able to frequently fly to California to visit his only son, daughter-in-law, and one grandchild, who was the apple of Leslie's eye. There was sympathy for the nice old man who'd lost his wife to cancer two years before relocating from Rhode Island to the DC area where he could enjoy the museums and beauty of the capitol city.

The reality of McCarter's life was somewhat different from what his neighbors knew.

Leslie McCarter, known in a different era as Staff Sergeant Leslie McCarter, was a decorated twenty-eight-year veteran of a little known military intelligence unit in the US Army. He had served for many years as a team leader of a small group of personnel who were assigned to the Fifth Special Forces Group of the army. He'd led a group of seven commandoes who at any given time would assist the Central Intelligence Agency and various other governmental agencies in removing obstacles, both human and otherwise, that might be blocking the door of democracy.

Oathmeyer had complete faith and affection for the retired sergeant. After all, it had been McCarter who'd led a team of "liberators" into a small apartment in Beirut, Lebanon, to rescue a young state department analyst named Leonard Oathmeyer, who in 1968 had been kidnapped by a small radical group of terrorists.

Leslie McCarter loved his retirement job. "Better than saying 'Welcome to

Wal-Mart,'" was his attitude toward sweeping Oathmeyer's problems out of the way.

Chapter 20

Nur and Kirk arrived within minutes of each other on the following Monday. They had time for coffee before the arrival of their transportation to an unknown location for training that hadn't been disclosed by their handler.

At exactly 9:00 a.m., "Joe" from Elite Limousine Service was waiting in the parking lot as Nur and Kirk walked from their office and entered the Lincoln Town Car. Joe smiled somewhat knowingly at Kirk as the two entered the car and the driver proceeded away from Washington, across the Fourteenth Street bridge, and toward Virginia.

Forty minutes later they arrived at the Central Intelligence Agency complex in Langley, where their training for the day would be held.

Before the occupants of the vehicle were allowed to enter the complex, they had to exit their car while it was being searched and provide their thumbprint from their right hands as they waited for the search to complete.

Upon having his thumbprint taken, Kirk noted that his picture, name, and employee number flashed on a screen. A group of color codes beneath the photograph indicated the level of security to which each person had been granted access and the reasons for being at the "farm" on that particular day.

When the search was finished, the three returned to their car, and Joe proceeded through the gate and down a series of paved roads that ended at a firing range.

For the next four hours, Nur and Kirk practiced and qualified with a new issue of a Glock 9mm handgun, which was said to be so advanced that the weapon would never activate a metal detector, no matter how sophisticated the detector was. Perhaps the most intriguing aspect of the weapon to Kirk and Nur was the fact that it was designed with a built-in noise suppressor and was even quieter than Senator Wingate's snoring during an emergency budgetary meeting.

Prior to departing the range, Chief, the firearms instructor, informed Nur and Kirk privately that they would probably be using the particular weapon in the near future.

They returned to the town car where Joe had been napping throughout the morning activities. The two were in their offices working on their planning phase within an hour.

That afternoon Lennie walked into their office and sat down for an unscheduled meeting with the two. "Let me know what you've accomplished so far," Oathmeyer stated.

For the next hour, Nur and Kirk discussed their activities, providing names, locations, and every trace of detail that had gone into their preparation.

"There is a home that's located at 12 Rue Duranti, in Paris," Lennie stated. "It's a safe house for you as well as the location where you not only can go for medical assistance, but you'll also go there for any weapon or any other piece of equipment you may need. You will knock on the front door of the residence exactly five times, and when the door is answered, you will state that you're a friend of the legion."

Oathmeyer also instructed the two that the occupants of the home spoke excellent English and would not ask any questions regarding the agents' assignment or any details at all relating to their presence in Paris. "They will simply supply and support," Lenny said.

The first step that Kirk and Nur made following their briefing was to access the virtual reality program and locate 12 Rue Duranti. Within an hour they had acquired the ability to locate the residence from any location in Paris. They specifically learned a series of routes in getting to or from the residence.

Kirk noted that in every sequence in which he traveled to or from Rue Duranti, there was a small blue Fiat, occupied by two males who were sitting inside the car, directly outside the residence.

Chapter 21

"Would you like to join me for dinner?" Kirk asked in Arabic, as he sat across from Nur.

"I'd absolutely love it," she replied with a smile.

The two had not had any type of social activity away from work since their training period in California, where they had combined incorporating the language training into sightseeing. It wasn't so much that they had not wanted to know each other socially as much as their desire to maintain a professional relationship. As it had turned out, the more that Nur and Kirk worked together, the stronger their friendship and confidence in each other became.

Lois Harding checked her watch when the two agents walked from the office together and left for the day. Lennie Oathmeyer had carefully spelled out several directives for Lois when she first assumed her administrative position at the BOP. Rule three on the lengthy list of employee responsibilities was to inform the director of any fraternization, no matter how innocent it may appear.

"Since you're going to become my bride in a few days, what would you like for dinner?" Kirk asked.

Nur smiled at his comment and immediately suggested that they go to a small Turkish restaurant that was within walking distance. "I've been dying for something from closer to home," she said.

The two were seated in a small, intimate booth that afforded the opportunity to converse in private. But after Nur spoke for a few minutes with a Turkish waiter in his native language, the waiter almost became a fixture of the table while trying to engage in conversation with Nur.

Kirk, with his knowledge of Arabic and almost no comprehension of

Turkish, was still able to understand the gist of the conversation between the two as they spoke of the area of Turkey that was bordered by Iraq.

"Can I assume that you are in fact from Zakho, or whatever that Kurdish town was where you lived?" Kirk asked.

Nur thought for a moment before responding. "Actually, everything I told you was the truth," she stated. "I'm just a poor Kurdish girl who found the American dream."

The dinner and conversation were both superb. The manager of the restaurant eventually admonished the waiter for socializing too much with the customers, and the two were then able to share and appreciate each other's company.

"What color level are you?" Nur asked. She was referring to a color code that was used in the intelligence service that designated just how far an employee could go in a conversation.

"I'm a blue, with a red stripe," Kirk responded.

The color coding system was simple when understood. First, an individual was never allowed to ask what color code the original requestor was. When asked, the recipient had to respond with their designated color. In this case, Nur knew that her assigned color was blue with a yellow stripe. Translated in the intelligence community, she was allowed to share any information with Kirk other than specific assignments she may have been involved in during her government service. As the senior classification, Nur immediately knew how far the conversation could be carried. Kirk, on the other hand, knew immediately the areas where he would not, could not, and definitely should not attempt to take the conversation.

The closeness of the two-color designations ensured the two could take the conversation much further than it sometimes could be taken, and fewer lies or cover stories were required.

After toasting over their second bottle of wine, they changed to Arabic and continued their conversation. Nur laughingly corrected some of the mispronunciations and ensured Kirk corrected his mistakes before continuing the dialogue.

"You're still an excellent teacher," Kirk stated.

"I was hoping to say those very words to you, but sometime later," she replied in a teasing but suggestive manner.

There was only a brief pause in the conversation when Kirk suddenly asked, "Nur, are we the only two 'employees' in the office?"

"Not at all," she responded. "I can't say how many, but there are more.

Everyone is currently working here and there, just trying to earn a buck for an honest day's work."

Kirk learned that there were many occasions where employees weren't in the office at all. In fact, there could be indefinite periods during which an employee wasn't seen or heard from, with the exception of briefing Lenny on his or her progress; in some isolated cases, the agent never returned to the office at all.

"We're never told directly when one of our own has met with fatal results. When Lenny has Lois clean out their desks, then we assume they won't be returning to work. It seems like a cold way of doing business," Nur noted, "but it's not a job for everyone, and sometimes an individual can't do the job."

Kirk fought the urge to continue asking questions and decided another topic could be more appropriate for the moment. Even Nur breathed a slight sigh of relief when the conversation reverted to topics that were more suitable to an after-dinner exchange.

As the two walked from the restaurant and returned to the Bureau of Prisons parking lot, Kirk asked Nur if she'd like to follow him to his apartment for coffee.

"I'd absolutely love to," she replied, "but big brother in that gray van across the street would undoubtedly pass it on to Lenny," she added.

Kirk had not noticed the vehicle in question, but when he casually looked, he noted the Ford van that had one occupant somewhat concealed in the front seat.

"Is this something I should grow to expect?" Kirk asked.

"Almost never, when you're on an assignment," Nur replied. "But when pursuing a social life, always expect that Lenny or one of his shadows will be hiding under the covers, or perhaps in a closet."

Kirk felt almost uncomfortable as the two parted company in the BOP parking lot and proceeded on their separate way.

As Kirk drove toward the Watergate, he noted a van that casually drove a block behind until he entered the underground parking area of his residence.

Leslie "The Broom" McCarter was only too glad to get back to Virginia. He had to make plans for a trip to Paris.

"Sometimes it's good to be a bit obvious," Leslie thought. "It keeps the kids on their toes and gets me an extra hour of sleep."

Chapter 22

"Well, how are my children doing today?" asked Lenny Oathmeyer as he walked into the office from his inner sanctum for a cup of coffee.

"Great," Nur responded. "We got a lot accomplished yesterday and then found a little Turkish restaurant for dinner."

Kirk could see the logic in Nur's confession by conversation. She was merely confirming to Lenny a fact of which he was already aware. He smiled and then returned to his office.

"Nice touch," said Kirk as he smiled across his desk at Nur.

"There's always Paris," she immediately retorted.

The preparation and planning continued with a daily review of all aspects of the assignment. Perhaps the only issue that was not resolved was the manner or technique that would be used to eliminate Al-Wakim.

Despite the fact that Lenny was able to provide a new video of their target as he arrived at his home, nothing at all was different from the scenario on the first video. When it came to arriving at his home, the terrorist was a creature of habit. Both Nur and Kirk knew that a creature of habit could prove to be very fatal to someone's health.

On April 3, Kirk, Nur, and Lenny met at the BOP office for a final briefing before their departure the following morning. The two would leave their cars in the office parking lot and would be taken to Dulles Airport for the departure.

Lenny then went over a checklist of questions and was satisfied with the efforts of his two associates. Lenny personally inspected the items or documents to ensure there were no mistakes.

"This son of a bitch deserves everything you're going to give him," Oathmeyer stated. "Just remember to take your time, do it right, do it effectively, and get the hell out of France as soon as possible. The president's best thoughts and well wishes are with you."

Kirk allowed himself to wonder privately whether or not the president of the United States was in fact aware of their assignment.

In truth, President Seymour D. Collier was not only aware of the assignment, but he'd also had his staff in the National Security Agency working for weeks on establishing a story of "plausible deniability" in the event that the operatives were apprehended or otherwise discovered.

The days of a spy carrying a cyanide capsule to end their life if they were captured was a thing of the past, fodder for spy novels. After all, Leslie McCarter knew his designated assignment as well as Kirk and Nur knew their own.

Chapter 23

Masoud Ali Al-Wakim truly enjoyed the life he'd carved for himself. As an individual who'd earned respect of others through meticulous planning, and with a daring to accomplish the impossible, he was revered and hated at the same time throughout a certain segment of the Middle East.

Masoud was a man who was truly feared throughout his own organization. He had no tolerance for failure by his followers and had proved throughout his life that success must be achieved not at *a* cost, but at *all* costs.

Having isolated himself in an area of Paris that was primarily frequented by faithful Muslims, Masoud had developed a certain amount of peace, serenity, and sense of well-being while riding through the streets of his neighborhood. He knew that within minutes of his own residence, he had the ability to summon at least fifty martyrs who would immediately sacrifice their lives for him or the cause.

Al-Wakim exercised every morning before his first bath of the day. This continued regimen throughout his life had ensured that at the age of fifty-four, he was in better physical condition than most men half his age.

He would be considered an empty nester by anyone who didn't know him, because he had no wife at home. Those who did know Masoud were only too aware that his wife had strapped explosives to her body and had walked into a club in Germany that was frequented by American servicemen who were celebrating week end passes. The list of suspects and organizations had been building for two years. With no remains that were identifiable, the martyrdom of Salim Al-Wakim was only known to a few. Masoud realized he didn't have to take credit when sometimes the slaughterer could remain unhunted and unwanted, giving them the opportunity to strike again.

Since the September 11 attacks in New York and Washington, Masoud had determined that his next act would not only exceed the work of his brothers in those attacks, but it would also exceed anything that had been accomplished in history. In reality, Masoud had personally provided counsel and expertise to four of the martyrs who'd completed their mission of Jihad on that.

Masoud Ali Al-Wakim lived in his small apartment with his faithful servant of twenty years, Hakim. His driver, Mohamed, had served him for five years, and Masoud knew that between the two, he was constantly surrounded by two of the most dedicated followers for which any man could ask. The fact that there were so many other followers within shouting range provided that extra degree of comfort that any hunted man would desire.

As time for his afternoon prayer approached, Masoud took his carpet and walked into the court of his backyard, where he could kneel and give thanks to Allah in private, for providing such a rewarding life.

Chapter 24

Kirk and Nur were pleasantly surprised when the ticket agent walked to the telephone public address system and announced that Flight 2027 would begin boarding for the flight to Paris, France, in just a few minutes.

Along with Kirk's fake passport and tickets for their flight was the used ticket from their purported flight from Richmond. Just like a true businessman, "Jeffrey" had kept the taxi receipt from his home in Richmond to that airport just to ensure his newspaper reimbursed him for every expense involved in the trip.

"I'm so glad I was able to get a copy of *Revenge Served Cold* at the book store," Nur stated. Her cover identity, "Cherise," was a devoted reader of anything written by her favorite author, Elmer L. Snow. She knew that the flight would go much faster, and with more intrigue, if she had something to read while airborne.

Kirk had been content to grab a copy of the *Washington Post*, which he would cram into his briefcase and wouldn't remove until they landed at Orly International ,where he could discard it on the seat of his plane.

They were soon waiting in line to enter the business class section of the aircraft for their journey abroad.

The previous day, Kirk and Nur had begun calling each other Jeff and Cherise. The day of practice had ensured their cover names were readily remembered.

The pilot announced their departure and invited the passengers to sit back and enjoy their flight. Kirk and Nur were more than happy to do just that.

An astute observer would have readily determined that the passengers in seats 27 A and B were more than content to just enjoy each other's company. They chatted frequently between themselves but were content not to move about the plane to engage in conversation with other passengers. One would have guessed, judging from their shiny wedding rings, that they were two newlyweds on their way to share their bodies with each other in Paris. One would only have guessed half right. They were en route to Paris but would only be sharing their expertise, not their bodies.

It was just a matter of hours until the soothing voice of the pilot advised his passengers that they were on a final approach to Orly International and would be landing in a matter of minutes.

The "Lonigans" were able to sense and share in the excitement as passengers began to prepare to land in the city of love. Despite their pending mission, Kurt and Nur were easily able to muster the same excitement and thrill of their pending landing as most of the other passengers.

"I just can't wait to get to the hotel and take a nice long bath," stated Nur.

Both maintained smiles on their faces as they walked through the terminal, retrieved their luggage, and processed through customs.

All paperwork was in order, and a smiling customs agent stamped their passports and instructed them in perfect English to enjoy their holiday.

Chapter 25

As the taxi passed the Eiffel Tower, the agents knew they were minutes from their hotel. In fact, Kirk was so familiar with the city from his training on the virtual reality program that he knew they would be at their hotel within two minutes. "Barring a terrorist attack," he thought.

There were no attacks, and within minutes Kurt and Nur were checking into the hotel and preparing to be escorted to their assigned room. The two had previously discussed their arrival and decided that their first night should be devoted to dinner and a glass of wine in the room.

A sign in the lobby prominently welcomed guests from the International Press and Media Association and informed them that free cocktails were available in the library bar.

"Want to glad-hand with some of your professional colleagues, big guy?" asked Nur as she nudged Kurt and pointed at the sign.

"Because I'm not in contention for a Pulitzer, I believe we should pass for the evening," he replied.

After a pleasant night in their room, Nur whispered good night as she glanced for the last time at the Eiffel Tower and then drifted into the peaceful world of sleep. Kirk elected to sleep on the couch.

Kirk woke first, ordered that coffee be sent to their room, and then called Lois Harding at a prearranged number in the states.

"News room," proclaimed Lois.

"This is Jeffrey," Kirk stated. "We've arrived and will start getting our feet wet this morning with the other newsmen."

"I would hope there are also newswomen there," Lois responded caustically before cheerfully giving a "be careful" and hanging up.

The two were soon enjoying their coffee before cleaning up and putting on casual clothing for a firsthand visit to the land of pending death.

Chapter 26

The two assassins left the hotel and walked to the area of Al-Wakim's home. They had previously determined that there was no need to visit their safe house until it had been determined what equipment or supplies they would need. Obviously, they wouldn't know what items would be needed until they had the opportunity to assess the situation.

It was virtual reality relived as they walked along the streets of Paris. The government operatives had a sense that they were as familiar with the area as anyone who'd lived there for their entire life.

"It's somewhat like déjà vu, isn't it?" Kirk stated.

"I was thinking the same thing," Nur replied.

As they approached Masoud's home at 110 Rue de la Roquette, it became more and more apparent that the two were entering some Middle Eastern country. Women were dressed in the "full covering" style with only their eyes visible. Men wore darker colors and beards, had mustaches, and appeared even more menacing. The spies began to feel they were being watched more closely and felt the first uncomfortable sensations since arriving the previous evening.

Nur and Kirk elected to terminate their walking surveillance and return to the area that was more inviting to tourists. The two had suddenly realized the difference in virtual reality and reality. In virtual reality, no one could see the two spies. In reality, they correctly felt the uncomfortableness of the situation.

They sought the seclusion of a small sidewalk café where they could enjoy coffee and assess their plans.

"I would suggest that one or both of us visit the safe house and arrange for a van and driver to take us through the neighborhood," Kirk stated.

"I agree," Nur's replied. "It may be best for you to be the one to go there to lessen the visibility of the two of us together."

The two then devised a list of items that would be needed immediately. Firearms, disguise kit for male and female, and most important a discreet van with a driver who had intimate knowledge of the city.

After formulating their immediate plans, they decided that Kirk would in fact go to the safe house alone, and Nur would visit some of the shops that were near, but not too near the area where they would be conducting their assignment. They had decided that Nur should purchase some clothing that was more appropriate for their operation area. The duo parted company and arranged to meet at their hotel room at 2:00 p.m.

Chapter 27

Kirk took a taxi from the café and instructed the driver to take him to the three hundred block of Rue Duranti. This would put him a good two blocks from the safe house and would ensure he could spot any surveillance he may have picked up prior to going to the house.

Ten minutes later his taxi dropped him off, and he casually took on the role of a sightseer as he aimlessly strolled down Rue Duranti, carefully looking in store windows that afforded him reflections of anyone in the surrounding area. Within minutes he had determined with a reasonable degree of certainty that he didn't have a tail on his movements and activities.

"He's good but needs a bit more training in counter surveillance," thought The Broom, who sat on a bench and ate an apple, just yards from Kirk's location.

As Kirk walked along the street toward the unit block, he observed the small blue Fiat, occupied by the two males, as it sat parked in front of the building. He walked up to the entrance of 12 Rue Duranti and knocked five times of the front door of the residence.

Kirk's intuition told him that weapons were pointed at his back while waiting for the door to open.

"I'm a friend of the Legion," Kirk stated as a short, overweight, elderly Frenchman opened the door and faced him.

The host smiled and faintly nodded approval in the direction of the two occupants of the Fiat.

"Monsieur, welcome, I'm Pierre," stated the smiling Frenchman as he opened the door wider and allowed Kirk to enter.

As Kirk walked into the foyer, he noted another male holding what appeared to be a British Sterling 9mm submachine gun as he retreated into a small room to the right of the hallway.

Kirk walked into a small living room and was offered hot tea, which he readily accepted. Nur had previously instructed Kirk, while training in California, that he should never refuse the gracious offer of hot tea.

Minutes later, Kirk was reciting his wish list to Pierre. Pierre memorized the requests that Kirk made and immediately pulled a cellular phone from his jacket pocket. After a short phone conversation, obviously made to a preprogrammed number, Pierre hung up the phone.

"Your supplies and vehicle will be here in thirty minutes," Pierre stated. "The driver of your van speaks excellent English and will be instructed to remain at your disposal throughout the assignment. For your convenience, there will be no need for you or any members of your team to return here unless you're injured. Now that we've established personal contact, your driver, Francois, will take any requests for supplies and will deliver them personally to you."

When a horn was heard from outside the home, Pierre stood and escorted his guest toward the front door.

"Viva les États-Unis," stated Pierre as Kirk walked into the sunlight and past the blue Fiat, entering a small, nondescript van that was double-parked in the street.

After introducing himself to Francois, they proceeded toward the Le Marquis Hotel. A black canvas bag that was placed between the two seats obviously contained the equipment that Kirk had requested.

"Could you pick up a colleague and me in two hours at the side entrance?" Kirk requested.

Francois confirmed he would be there.

Kirk walked into the front entrance of the hotel and proceeded to his room to meet with his partner.

Nur's shopping excursion had taken less time than Kirk's, and she was in the bathroom when he returned to the room. "Be out in just a few," she yelled.

Kirk saw numerous shopping bags lying on the bed and throughout the room. He placed the canvas duffle bag that he'd received from Francois on a table and began removing the contents. Two Glock automatic pistols with ten fully loaded clips, three spare boxes of ammunition, a pair of binoculars with night vision capabilities, four disposable cellular phones, a roll of duct tape, and two kits that contained professional makeup and disguises. Although he hadn't requested them, there were two shoulder holsters, fully adjustable and designed to hold the weapon close to the body to eliminate bulges. The guns were identical to the ones that he and Nur had recently qualified with at CIA Headquarters. Kirk noted that there wasn't a bit of metal on the holsters, which indicated that he and Nur could carry their firearms through any metal detectors they encountered in Paris.

"I feel like I'm back in Zakho," said Nur as she walked from the bathroom.

Kirk was amazed at the transformation. His partner was wearing the traditional Muslim prayer outfit that covered her from head to toe. With the exception of her eyes, Nur was fully concealed inside the outfit. Nur's naturally dark eyebrows only emphasized that she was Middle Eastern, Muslim, and ready to walk anywhere without raising suspicions of those whom she was born near but had learned to hate.

As the two went from shopping bag to shopping bag, Kirk noted the hijabs and scarves of various colors, which could be used to partially or fully cover Nur's face.

Nur noted, but would not touch, a small red vial that was inside the supplies that Kirk had retrieved.

"That part of the assignment is strictly for the male reporter," she stated with a smile.

Kirk nodded in acknowledgment.

Chapter 28

At exactly 2:00 p.m. the two assassins entered the van, and Francois drove them from the hotel area. They proceeded to the area of Square de la Rogette, where Francois pulled into the parking area, and the three programmed their cellular phones with each other's number. The darkly tinted windows and magnetic sign on the side of the van that identified the vehicle as a flower delivery device ensured no one paid a bit of attention to the vehicle or occupants.

Kirk noted that the back of the vehicle contained video equipment, numerous magnetic signs, and sets of license plates that could transform the vehicle into any type of a service truck at a moment's notice. He wondered if this very vehicle had been used to document the virtual reality videos that had been so instrumental in the planning process. No matter; as the quick preparation and briefing period concluded, the van began moving, and Kirk and Nur relived the many trips they'd made through this area of Paris through the virtual reality program.

The team made numerous trips past their target residence at 110 Rue de la Roquette. Because it was not at all unusual in Paris for flower delivery drivers to utilize alleys, they were never given a second glance as Kirk and Nur saw in person the area where they would hopefully complete their mission.

The small courtyard in the rear of Masoud's residence presented an excellent point for attack. Although the yard was surrounded by a stone fence, it was low enough for an agile attacker to transgress the wall and be inside the area in just a moment.

After consulting with Nur, the two decided that they'd spent enough time circling the neighborhood in the van. Francois would drop Nur off a few blocks from the residence and she, in her prayer outfit, would conduct surveillance from the ground.

Nur had concealed her weapon under the prayer dress before leaving the hotel. Kirk took a small piece of duct tape and, after ensuring that Nur's phone was on a vibrating mode, taped the phone to the calf of her right leg.

"I'm sure glad I shave my legs," she joked as he applied the tape.

After establishing that Nur would meet the van at the square following her mission, she was dropped at a remote area but within minutes of Al-Wakim's home. Any phone contact, even a ringing of the phone, would indicate a call for immediate assistance from Kirk.

Kirk felt apprehensive as the van drove away, and yet he reminded himself that Nur was a fully qualified equal, trained in her craft and mandated to accept the risks that any operative in the world may be expected to assume.

Francois showed the first indication of an in-depth knowledge of human behavior when he said to Kirk, "Don't worry, mon ami, I've already noted that your partner is a true professional."

The two waited at the park for two hours before they observed Nur walking in their direction with several plastic shopping bags of fruits and vegetables.

"It was quite interesting," stated Nur as she entered the van and directed Francois to return them to the hotel. She did not discuss any details during the ride and limited her conversation to small talk related to the beauty of Paris.

On arrival at the hotel, Nur gave her purchases to Francois, and the three decided that future contact would be made via phone, at a time the agents deemed appropriate.

Chapter 29

Because of the contradictions in their manner of dress, Nur and Kirk chose to enter their hotel through different directions to ensure they weren't observed together. They would meet at their room.

Ten minutes later the two sat in their room and began a debriefing of their day's activities. They started with their exercise from leaving their room at the beginning of the day and methodically discussed every detail until their return.

The two immediately decided that instead of going out as "typical" Americans who were enjoying their holiday, they would leave and return to the hotel separately. The agents also decided that they would meet Francois further away from the hotel, which might provide a bit more anonymity and cover for their assignment.

Both had noted the potential of utilizing the rear area of Masoud's home as a logical site to commit themselves to their task at hand. Nur had noted that a small hotel that was located to the East of Al-Wakim's home had a view, at least from the eighth floor and up, of the courtyard area of the target's home.

"Don't forget," said Nur, "Masoud's prayer means he must face the sun, and so he is looking east during his morning prayer. This would put a limit on his view because of the bright sun, and it would enhance our own line of sight while providing us distance."

The logic of her comments truly impressed Kirk as he mulled over the content of her suggestion.

As the sequence of events progressed and the topic approached Nur's solo sojourn while on foot, Kirk became astounded at her report.

"I spotted at least fifteen men and women, some or all of who form a protective ring around our target's home on Rue de la Roquette." She then pulled a piece of paper from her folder and quickly sketched a map of the area. After doing so, Nur precisely identified the suspected terrorists by sex and description, described what apparent role they played in the neighborhood, and showed their location.

Kirk mentally noted the comments, locations, descriptions, and details that his partner had provided.

"Look at this!" Kirk stated. He took Nur's map and made two circles around the home of Masoud. The circles revealed two almost concentric rings that surrounded the home. "Masoud has two rings of security whose job is to surround his home and provide perimeter protection," he noted.

The assassins discussed the situation for several hours before deciding on the next step of their plan. The International Press and Media Association would not have been happy to know that one of their members would possibly be making news instead of reporting news.

That very afternoon, an irate "Cherise Lonigan" contacted the Hotel de la Mer, which was located at 136 Rue de la Folie Regnault. She explained to the sympathetic desk clerk how she and her husband had found the accommodations at Le Marquis Hotel completely intolerable.

"I can live with filth, but I absolutely refuse to share my room with cockroaches," Cherise stated.

Unfortunately, the Hotel de la Mer did not have a room on the ninth floor that had a view of the Eiffel Tower, but they had an available suite on the tenth floor that afforded an even better view. The Lonigans of Virginia would be arriving within the hour.   The desk clerk of the Le Marquis was only too sad to hear that the Lonigans were returning to the United States because of a family emergency. He quickly prepared the bill and wished the two a safe journey as their luggage was carried to a waiting taxi.

The taxi driver looked sad when his instructions were changed by Kurt to take them to the Hotel de la Mer, rather than Orly International Airport; the new destination was a shorter, less expensive trip. However, his attitude changed when he received a substantial gratuity upon arrival at the couple's new hotel.

As the Lonigans entered room 1006 in their new hotel, Cherise thought she observed a cockroach as it scurried from view. Nonetheless, the room appeared perfect for their needs, including an outstanding view of more than just the Eiffel Tower; there was a view of a nice little apartment with a beautiful courtyard in the rear.

After the Lonigans showered and dressed, they walked to a small, intimate French restaurant that was within walking distance of their new hotel, and they enjoyed excellent French cuisine.

Meanwhile, Masoud Ali Al-Wakim sat in the modest living room of his home with three of his most trusted confidantes and discussed ways in which American corporations could be brought to their knees.

Chapter 30

Nur and Kirk had decided the vantage point of their new room provided such an excellent view of Masoud's home that they would conduct surveillance from that location for the foreseeable future.

Nur had placed a "Do Not Disturb" sign on the door of their room before they went to bed, and Kirk had initiated a surveillance that had started at 5:00 a.m. By agreement between the two, Kirk would maintain surveillance while Nur, dressed in her prayer outfit, would repeat her travels from the previous day. They agreed that each perspective would give them a clearer and more precise picture that would assist in their planning.

At precisely 6:00 a.m., a lone figure came into view in the rear of 110 Rue de la Roquette. Through his binoculars, Kirk had a perfect view of Masoud Ali Al-Wakim as he placed a small prayer rug onto the ground. Masoud then removed his sandals, stood straight as he peered toward the east, and after several moments kneeled to the ground.

"Nur, take a look at this," Kirk excitedly exclaimed.

She immediately jumped from the bed and stood silently behind Kirk as she saw the distant figure of their quarry as he engaged in his morning ritual of prayer. "It's a perfect line of sight," she whispered.

After several minutes, Al-Wakim stood, put his sandals back on, and proceeded back into the residence.

Prior to Nur's departure from the room, she removed the duct tape from the travel bag and carefully taped the cellular phone to her calf. A short time later the Muslim guest of the hotel walked toward Rue de la Roquette, being watched closely through binoculars that were concealed inside room 1006.

After evaluating the potential for a hit being conducted from the confines of their room, Kirk determined that although extremely thick, a portion of the window could be removed with a glass cutter. He also recognized that the distance between his room and Al-Wakim's courtyard was well within the range of his ability to fire a fatal rifle shot from his vantage point.

The negative aspect of using room 1006 was the fact that a hole in the window, associated with an assassination within view, would ensure that local law or intelligence officials would quickly determine that Jeffrey and Cherise Lonigan of Richmond, Virginia, would most assuredly be caught before they could fly out of the country.

Kirk knew that this issue would be a major topic of discussion that evening between himself and Nur. Throughout his career in training for this type of situation, Kirk recognized that he was only facing a slight barrier, not a brick wall.

At 12:00 p.m., Kirk used his cellular phone to contact Lois Harding on the assigned number at the Bureau of Prisons.

"Newsroom, how may I help you?" asked Lois.

"This is Jeffrey," Kirk stated. "Everything is going better than expected. The conference should be over in a couple of days, and barring unforeseen delays we should be home soon." Kirk added a final message before the call was terminated. "On the final; go one up from the last on the other."

"I got it, and enjoy the conference," Lois stated.

Within ten minutes Kirk realized that the National Security Agency would be monitoring his and Nur's every move.

Through his encrypted message, Lois had understood that "on the final; go one up from the last on the other" were instructions to take the number on the caller ID that Kirk was calling from and program it. Then, add one digit to the last number on Kirk's phone, which would provide both phone numbers that were being used by the agents.

When Lois informed Oathmeyer that the situation was operational, Lenny went to a secure site on his computer, and in real time he saw a map of Paris that revealed the precise location where each agent was situated.

"How in the hell did we survive before the computer age?" thought Oathmeyer.

After establishing contact via computer monitoring, Lennie called Senator Wingate on his private and very secure phone. He relayed the message that Lois had received and the fact that both operatives were on the screen and within minutes of their target destination.

Nur returned to the hotel within an hour. She had discarded her purchases with the exception of fresh apples, which she thought might be tasty snacks during the surveillance.

As was standard with the two, they sat while watching Masoud's home from a distance and discussed the chronological events thus far that day.

"I'm glad you passed our grid lines on to Lois," Nur stated. "I should have thought of that yesterday, but because we were only working peripherally, I didn't really see the need, then."

Nur's walking surveillance had reduced the number of suspected terrorists in the concentric circle to twelve.

"This location and that one were missing today," she stated while pointing at the map she'd drawn the previous day.

Nur did not feel there was any suspicious behavior that would indicate that their target or his security agents were aware of her presence in the neighborhood. She also agreed with Kirk on his own assessment for using their room as the point of initiating the anticipated kill.

"Perhaps we should have brought documents with a second identity for our transfer from the Le Marquis to here," Nur suggested. "There's just no way we can use this room and have the hit linked back, either officially or unofficially, to our country. It's a shame we didn't arrive at this hotel with Iranian passports, take him out, and allow Allah to sort through the details."

Chapter 31

Had Nur and Kirk known more about the intricacies of neighborhood protocol in the small Muslim enclave of Paris, their entire planning procedure may well have changed.

Al-Wakim and his security advisors had long ago established a neighborhood policy where women who were covered weren't always recognizable by the area inhabitants. Females were taught from their youth that whenever a veiled woman crossed a certain faded line of paint on the sidewalks surrounding Rue de la Roquette, they would open and close their right hand twice as they crossed the designated line. This subtle gesture ensured that certain well-armed street vendors, who were assigned to look for such signals, were able to distinguish between the area residents, an occasional visitor, or an infidel who may be prone to creating problems in the close-knit neighborhood.

When a veiled woman crossed the line once without giving the signal, it was a "forgot." When that individual crossed the line twice without giving a signal, it was a "coincidence," and when it happened for a third time, it was a "trespass."

The locals had no love or affection for trespassers.

Nur's travels through the area, although appreciated by local merchants, had already become a "coincidence."

Chapter 32

The operatives decided to have dinner in their room. They were close to fatigue, which was more mental than physical.

Kirk had shared with Nur that during her absence that day, Masoud had walked into his courtyard several times where he repeated his religious prayers. This was the only period of the day when the target was obviously unguarded and spent his time with Allah alone.

Nur, on the other hand, had witnessed their target leaving his residence and subsequently returning. "His patterns were exactly as they were in our surveillance videos," she stated.

With the availability of the night vision device that was an integral part of the binoculars, Kirk and Nur took turns while sitting in their darkened room as they watched for activity at the home of Al-Wakim. The interior lights of the home were extinguished at 10:00 p.m., and the two agents elected to take the opportunity to get a good night of sleep.

At 5:00 a.m., Kirk sat quietly at the window and watched the traffic of Paris as it began to get into motion. There was no need to use the binoculars because his view was more of a general nature, and there was no immediate need to close in for a specific view.

Nur slept comfortably in her own bed. Kirk was not accustomed to spending nights with a beautiful woman with no fringe benefits.

At precisely 6:00 a.m., Masoud Ali Al-Wakim came into view in the courtyard of his residence. He carefully placed his prayer carpet on the ground, stood facing the east, and then removed his sandals. Within moments, Masoud was kneeling and performing the ritual of his first prayer of the day.

After a period of time, Masoud returned to his feet, faced east for a full two minutes, and then replaced his sandals and walked out of view toward the rear door of his home.

Kirk made notations on a small pad to document the activities he'd just observed.

Kirk spent his peaceful morning watching the neighborhood as its inhabitants awoke, and he decided to order coffee and juice so that he and Nur could have a few minutes of social time before they decided what course they would take during the day.

An hour later Nur had finished her shower, and the two sat by the window having croissants and coffee and discussing the plans for the day.

Nur and Kirk held a lengthy conversation about their activities for the past three days. They agreed that Masoud had demonstrated a pattern at a time in which he was extremely vulnerable and in a time frame when there was little likelihood of an innocent being injured.

"We would be absolutely hung out to dry if we injured or killed a noncombatant," Nur stated.

Kirk nodded in total agreement.

They finally decided that the following morning, when Masoud conducted his 6:00 a.m. prayer, would be the ideal time to complete their assignment. The agents worked throughout the morning as they implemented their surveillance activities into a workable plan.

"Let's not overlook the two guards that stand on the corner," Nur stated. "They're actually the only members of the concentric ring from which we must anticipate resistance. The rest are along the street in front of the house."

Nur made the call to Lois Harding and instructed her that the following morning the two had an extremely important meeting at 6:00 a.m. She also advised Lois that they would be returning home quickly after the meeting as possible.

"I wish you both the safest of journeys," said Lois. "I'll make sure the editor is aware of your plans."

Lennie Oathmeyer, was immediately notified of the planned operation. He in turn sent a text message to The Broom to ensure he would be available for support or any other reason in which his expertise might be needed.

Nur contacted the airlines and was able to reserve two business class seats for an 11:35 a.m. departure from Orly to Dulles the following day.

The final call was to Francois, who'd started to wonder why he hadn't heard from the two American compatriots. Francois readily agreed to meet the couple in their hotel room that evening at 6:15 regarding what had been described to him as a big event. Kirk listed a few items that he requested Francois bring with him when he came to the room.

When the residents of the Muslim neighborhood didn't see the unknown female for the third day in a row, there was a collective sigh of relief.

Masoud Ali Al-Wakim had been informed of the presence of a new person in the area who also wasn't aware of the protocol expected of area residents. He'd instructed his personnel to take her into custody if she returned and bring her to him for a proper interrogation. It wasn't so much that sirens and whistles were being sounded, however; Masoud had not remained alive for fifty-four years by being stupid.

Chapter 33

The meeting with Francois the previous evening had gone very well. He'd brought the new supplies the clandestine team would need, and at the request of Kirk and Nur, he had taken some of the supplies they would no longer need as he departed.

The two had only shared such details that Francois would absolutely need to know in his providing assistance for the two Americans. In their preparations, Kirk had contacted the front desk of the hotel and arranged for an express checkout the following morning. The final statement would be billed to the credit card of Jeffrey C. Lonigan and left under the entrance door of the room. Jeffrey would sign the bill and leave a copy at the desk on their way out of the hotel.

Kirk and Nur had worked late into the night on discussing the "what ifs" of their plan. When they went to bed, both were well versed on how the operation would be carried out.

Many government agencies from around the world would have been shocked that only two agents were being utilized to eliminate a terrorist whose very name sent shivers up the spines of their undercover assets. The various intelligence agencies of the US government had met to discuss this very issue. It had been decided that a trial program should be conducted where measures of success would be considered along with the number of personnel involved and the objectives being met. Thus far the experiment had worked extremely well in that several persons of interest had been located, identified, and eliminated. No government agents had been lost or their identity compromised during these assignments. The US intelligence community had made a correct assessment. If a handful of terrorist could bring a country to its knees with a small group, a small cell of freedom fighters could do the same.

Chapter 34

At 5:10 a.m., Kurt and Nur walked out of the elevator, accompanied by the bellboy they'd summoned to handle their luggage.

Kurt walked to the front desk and handed over his signed copy of the hotel bill. Nur proceeded to the hotel entrance with their luggage. The luggage was quickly loaded into the side door of a small van that displayed signage indicating it was an Orly Airport shuttle. Jeffrey tipped the doorman, and the taxi departed for the airport.

As the taxi left the hotel, Nur immediately opened a small suitcase and removed a black prayer dress. At the same time, Kirk opened his own valise, changing clothes and applying makeup.

Francois drove aimlessly as the two prepared for their morning activities.

At 5:56 a.m., a Muslim woman, dressed in her religious attire and pushing a wheelchair, walked slowly up Rue de la Roquette. The wheelchair held an elderly Middle Eastern male whose bright white beard reflected in the predawn glow of the rising sun.

There was nothing at all unusual about the scene. In fact, this was an almost daily occurrence in the neighborhood, with the exception that the morning stroll was a bit earlier than normal. Nevertheless, it was a pattern that blended completely with the character of the neighborhood and didn't raise an iota of suspicion.

Sirens could be heard in the distance as they headed away from the neighborhood. There had just been a report that a police officer had been shot approximately four miles away. Every officer in the area had been dispatched to assist their fallen comrade. Law enforcement wouldn't be an impediment for the foreseeable time span.

Out of the corner of his eye, Kirk noted Al-Wakim as he walked to his normal courtyard prayer spot from the rear of his home. The assassins had what they'd determined to be a two-minute window of opportunity to complete their mission.

The terrorists nearest the home of Masoud glanced in their direction as they came into view. Nur proceeded a bit faster while pushing the wheelchair to a predetermined point, at which time the elderly man jumped from the wheelchair and began running toward the courtyard.

Kirk ran quickly and silently past the two terrorists, giving wide berth to ensure he remained outside a line of fire. The terrorists noted movement, and although startled, their reactions were remarkably quick. Not quite quick enough, though, because Nur had drawn her weapon from a concealed location on the wheelchair and was already pulling the trigger.

As Kirk vaulted the fence, both security men, now standing behind him, were already falling to the ground, now completely lifeless from well-placed bullets in their heads and an additional two bullets in their hearts.

Nur left the wheelchair in its place, and as she ran past the two bodies, she fired an additional guarantee shot into each of the torsos.

Masoud had been halfway to his knees when he was distracted by a repetition of puffs that were resultant from Nur's firing of her silencer equipped Glock. As Masoud looked, a bearded male holding a handgun landed on the ground inside the fenced compound.

Kirk immediately turned to his left and fired three shots dead center through the glass door of the residence. He noted a figure as he was falling from view.

Kirk then turned to Masoud while saying in Arabic, "The President of the United States sends his regards."

Before firing the six bullets that would ensure Masoud Ali Al-Wakim never would dream of, plan, or participate in another terrorist act, Kirk produced a small red vial and threw the contents onto Masoud.

"I hope you enjoy having the blood of a pig on your body," Kirk stated.

As the dying Masoud gasped the final breath of his life, he fully realized that the blood of the pig would ensure he not only would never find Allah, but also that those promised virgins would never be touched by his dead hands.

Kirk was immediately back across the fence where Nur, who'd assumed a combat firing position, protected his flank from the chance of someone running into view to provide assistance to the terrorists.

A taxi immediately stopped by the fence, and the two entered the vehicle, which quickly sped away. The sound of an AK-47 could be heard as someone inside the house returned fire at the fleeing assailants.

As the taxi left the area, Kirk threw the glass vial to the pavement, breaking it into thousands of pieces, thus ensuring no fingerprints would be found.

Before reaching the airport, Nur, Kirk, and Francois abandoned their taxi for a clean vehicle. While grabbing their luggage, Kirk noted three holes in the trunk of the vehicle that had been fired from the automatic weapon inside the residence. They were scarcely a block away from the taxi when it suddenly exploded. It was a fire fueled by accelerants and would completely burn the prayer dresses, disguises, and any evidence that may have been inside the taxi van.

The crime scene where Masoud had been terminated would reveal some significant evidence, particularly a wheelchair whose handles were coated by a type of tape that wouldn't provide fingerprints.

Perhaps the best information that the criminal investigation division of the Paris police department would produce was the statement of an eye witness, a newspaper reporter from the Associated Press in Ankara, Turkey. That eye witness, who was attending the International Press and Media Association Conference, stated that the two suspects appeared to be of Middle Eastern descent, because of their dress.

The Turkish reporter's vantage point was from the thirteenth floor of Hotel de la Mer.

When the ballistics specialists of the criminal investigations bureau examined the empty projectiles from the guns, they determined that the statement of the eye witness was definitely credible. The ammunition used in the killing of Al-Wakim and his associates had been produced by an Iranian company in Tehran.

Chapter 35

Prior to departing Orly for their return travel to the United States, Nur contacted their office. "Please advise the editor that the conference has been successfully completed, and we're returning home," Nur stated.

While the two employees of the Bureau of Prisons were resting comfortably as they flew across the Atlantic toward Washington, a previously unknown Iranian terrorist organization was contacting Middle Eastern news outlets and taking credit for the assassination of a former Iranian citizen, Masoud Ali Al-Wakim.

Although they were pretty much exhausted from their assignment, both operatives felt a keen sense of relief and a strong feeling of satisfaction in their accomplishment. Four terrorists were dead, including a major source of danger to all citizens of the United States in particular and citizens of the world in general.

While the agents were involved in their planning, a review of comprehensive intelligence that had been collected by so many various agencies through several years had revealed Al-Wakim's suspected or confirmed connection to dozens of acts of terrorism that had cost the lives of many innocents.

Nur knew from her extensive experience that government intelligence would be closely monitoring computer and international phone chatter by now. Any call or e-mail made or sent from a certain area in Paris would be closely monitored with precise records maintained of numbers called or recipients of the mail.

When something "big" occurs in the world of terrorism and intelligence, numerous government agencies go into full speed in grasping any bit of information that could lead a government to their next target. Nur was completely aware that through the efforts of herself and Kirk. something big had indeed happened.

In his private office at the Bureau of Prisons, Leonard Oathmeyer returned to his desk with a fresh cup of coffee and sat down. A quick check of his computer on the NSA-provided website showed that his two agents were just off the coast of Newfoundland.

Chapter 36

The following Monday morning, Nur and Kirk returned to their office. They were prepared for a full week that would be mentally taxing, nerve-racking, and somewhat harassing.

Intelligence protocol dictated that following certain assignments, the operatives who had participated in the operation would be separated and required to prepare concise, individual reports that registered the facts of the operation they'd conducted.

The agents were not only required to provide reports that were accurate down to the smallest details, but they were also required to add footnotes that recorded the logic behind certain decisions as well as what personal feelings they might recall that reflected their decisions. Analysts would evaluate the information, search for new leads for further investigations and assignments, and pass copies of the report of activities on to psychologist and psychiatrists, who would evaluate the personal feelings of the operatives and attempt to determine any negative mental issues that might require treatment.

The final process would be a polygraph examination, the questions being formed from the reports, and would be directed at any breach of security the operatives may have been involved in but hadn't reported.

Leslie "The Broom" McCarter, unknown to Kirk and Nur, had flown back to the United States on the next flight. His verbal and written report would shed one piece of light on the abilities of the two operatives. "They're just about as proficient in their craft as any team I've ever worked with or supervised or clandestinely monitored," Leslie stated in his official report.

By the end of the week, all paperwork had been completed and filed.

The operation was rated with such a high level of importance and success that, through a conference call, Senator Royal T. Wingate informed Kirk and Nur the president had asked him to convey his congratulations for their dedicated service to their country. No reference was made to the events leading to, during, or following their display of dedicated service. "Kind of like my service record," Kirk thought as he remembered his army discharge. "Everything was done, yet nothing was officially recorded."

On Friday afternoon, Kirk was sitting in his office when a new face came through the door of his office accompanied by Lennie.

"Kirk, I want you to meet one of the more experienced members of our team," Lennie stated. "This is Frank Gale, who has just returned from a four-month assignment."

Kirk immediately stood to shake hands with a smiling Frank Gale. "I was beginning to think there were no other employees working out of this office," Kirk joked.

"Frank has been recuperating from a few injuries and will be working with you on your next assignment. I'll let you two get acquainted," he said as he walked back toward his office.

Chapter 37

Kirk immediately liked Frank. They determined that they both held color codes of blue, with a red stripe. In short, the two had equal access to the same levels of security, and neither would be restricted to topics of discussion.

Frank was thirty-six years old and a native of Knoxville, Tennessee. He had a youthful face and a perfect smile, and the closeness of his blonde hair would have given anyone the impression that he was a soldier. In fact, he had previously been assigned to the Fifth Special Forces Group and had been stationed at Fort Bragg, North Carolina.

"I spent fourteen years at Bragg making sure that every morning my foot locker had six pairs of display socks that I couldn't wear, a toothbrush and razor I never used but that were always pointed in the right direction, and my highly shined boots that I never wore were prominently displayed under my bunk," Frank stated.

"Too much bullshit for me," Kirk said with a smile as he recalled his own experiences in the military.

Frank wasn't married but stated that he did have a former wife who was probably lying on some California beach and profiling her assets like a silicone goddess. "I've been dating a young administrative assistant from the Supreme Court," Frank added. "She has a passion for the law, yet she's not opposed to breaking the law by getting naked and driving with me to Ocean City." He laughed. "Perhaps you'd like to date Sandra Day O'Connor. I can hook you two up in minutes."

Frank Gale appeared not to have a single worry in the world, which was true.

Unknown to Kirk, his new friend had just spent four months in

Walter Reed Army Hospital in Bethesda, Maryland, where he'd undergone extensive treatment for severe injuries that had been caused by an improvised exploding device in Balad, Iraq. Gale had been working under the cover of KBR, a subsidiary of Halliburton Corporation, when the device exploded. The incident convinced him that timing isn't just anything—it's everything.

When Frank had finally been convinced that he would make a full recovery, he decided that life was indeed great and refused to let his mind wander to any issue that was out of his immediate control.

"Kirk, we all know how much money we have, but we never know how much time is left to spend it," Gale stated. "My philosophy is spending it as fast as you earn it."

Lois Harding, who was near Kirk's office, heard Frank's reference to spending. "It's great to have him back," Lois thought as she mentally repeated the statement to ensure she'd have something profound to say at her next bridge club gathering.

Kirk was enjoying the company of his fellow operative so much that he didn't hesitate when Frank invited him to grab a beer before calling it a day.

The two closed the bar of Georgetown's Foggy Bottom Bar before prudently deciding to take cabs to their respective homes.

"Thank God for weekends," thought Kirk as he turned out the light and ignored setting his alarm.

He slept late the following morning before getting up and taking a six-mile run to the Capitol and returning to the Watergate complex.

By Monday morning he felt like a new man and was anxious for Lenny to give him his new assignment.

Chapter 38

Leonard Oathmeyer had been contacted early on Saturday morning and summoned to the CIA headquarters in Langley, Virginia, for an 11:30 meeting. This wasn't an unusual occurrence because weekends were frequently used for intelligence briefings. Lennie was somewhat surprised when he noted that Senator Wingate was also attending. The senator usually received his briefings at a significantly higher level. "Something is in the works," Oathmeyer thought.

Matthew Hellerman, the director of the CIA, chaired the meeting, which was attended by senior representatives from CIA, NSA, FBI, the attorney general, and the secretary of state.

"Gentlemen, we're here because of a matter of grave importance in defending our national security," Hellerman stated. "I'm going to ask Director Sanders of the FBI to bring you up to speed."

As Sanders walked to the podium of the small conference room, he briefly smiled in the direction of Oathmeyer.

"A few days ago," Sanders said, "a government team conducted an assignment in Paris, France, under the direction of Leonard Oathmeyer. Unfortunately, as so often happens in our business, a radical Iranian group is getting the accolades and praise. Our team was successful in eliminating their target, Masoud Ali Al-Wakim, however, there was an unexpected bonus that we'd not anticipated. A second individual, who was not known to be inside the residence, was also eliminated. Our operatives not only terminated Al-Wakim, but they also killed his superior, Yasin Mohamed Tikriti. Reviews of all submitted documents indicate that Tikriti was standing inside a back door of the residence, and although not recognized, he was perceived as a threat that had to be neutralized by our operative.

Next we can concentrate on Osama Bin Laden. All in all, not a bad day for the United States of America," he stated.

There was a sudden outburst of applause as the gathered leaders of the intelligence community realized that Osama Bin Laden's second in command had been taken out.

The briefing only got better as Sanders continued.

"Following the completion of the operation, the NSA began an aggressive monitoring of all computer and phone chatter originating in certain areas of Paris. A most interesting notification was made from a phone in Paris to a small town, Pigeon Forge, Tennessee. As most of you may know, Pigeon Forge is located at the entrance to the Smoky Mountain National Park, next to Gatlinburg.

"Our analysts feel with almost certainty that an Al-Qaeda cell that is active, or possibly a sleeper cell, is in that area—which by the way hosts over eleven million tourists a year. You can just imagine the impact an act of terrorism would have at the doorway of one of our national parks.

"We have identified the recipient of the Paris call and, through electronic surveillance, have located four other people in Pigeon Forge or Gatlinburg, who are conversing in Arabic. Although their calls are coded, we know that these individuals are what some would describe as 'madder than a wet hen.'" Sanders ended his conversation with a statement of cold reality. "The enemy feels with certainty that the recent retribution in Paris was based on orders, and perhaps operatives from the US government, and we must be more vigilant than at any time since September 11."

The meeting lasted for several hours as the group made decisions on the logistical approach that might be used to confront terrorists in the very heart of Tennessee.

Before the meeting adjourned, Lenny Oathmeyer was called on to provide details of the assignment in Paris. He remained politically correct throughout his talk by sharing the credit with all gathered agencies because all of the agencies had, in fact, contributed extensive intelligence that had enabled the operation to be initiated, planned, and successfully concluded without the loss of life or injury to any American operatives or foreign personnel who'd been recruited to assist the team from the American government.

"We all must realize," Lenny said in conclusion, "that we're only as good as the assignment we complete today, not for the one we finished yesterday, and tomorrow remains to be resolved."

Senator Royal T. Wingate nodded his head knowingly when this statement was made.

Chapter 39

On Sunday afternoon, Kirk received a phone message from Oathmeyer that instructed him to ensure he was at the office by 8:30 am the following day. Frank Gale had received a similar message.

Lennie then worked well into the evening engaging in conference calls with several of the same colleagues he'd met with during the previous day's meeting at CIA Headquarters.

Ironically, prior to September 11, Oathmeyer would rarely have direct contact with other agency heads. Intelligence information would be forwarded to the National Security Agency, who would filter the intelligence to a designated agency that was responsible for the particular geographical area or whose operatives handled the particular type of case. The Federal Bureau of Investigation would have been the lead agency on any domestic security issue that may have surfaced. On the flip side of the coin, the Central Intelligence Agency would have directed their efforts to problems that were occurring on foreign soil. Not only were all intelligence agencies now working closely, but they were also joined by the Department of Homeland Security, who was now a member of the team and had become a contributor of outstanding intelligence information that related to the constant coming and going of foreigners into and out of the United States.

Through close coordination between the agencies on Sunday, all departments were aware of the direction they would be taking the assignment when their own operatives were briefed on the following day. Monday would be a busy day in the area of Washington DC, with many new faces heading to the hills of the Great Smoky Mountains.

Chapter 40

Kirk and Frank met in the parking lot as they arrived for work on Monday. While attempting to maneuver through thousands of pedestrians who were heading past the reflecting pool near the Lincoln Memorial, Kirk remembered that it was the day when thousands of illegal aliens from Mexico were marching on the Capitol and petitioning their rights to citizenship, employment, and a host of other demands.

"Can you believe this crap?" Frank asked as the two walked toward their private entrance of the Federal Bureau of Prisons. "The last time we had so many pissed-off non-citizens marching on Washington and under the flag of another nation was when the British burned Washington on August 24, 1814."

Kirk was impressed that his new friend had a grasp of history and was able to recall dates so quickly. "I have trouble remembering my own birth date," Kirk thought.

The two grabbed a cup of coffee, which had already been prepared by Lois Harding, and walked to Lenny's office.

"Come on in, guys. it's going to be the first of many long days," Oathmeyer stated.

As the two CIA operatives listened to Lenny, other operatives at Langley, as well as agents from the FBI and National Security, received similar briefings from their own handlers and supervisors.

"I sent Nur back to Paris yesterday morning, and she will be assisting in performing leg work in that area," Lenny stated. "Besides Frank, she's the most up-to-date of our operatives and will maintain a command post in the hotel where you both stayed. She will be assisted by personnel who are already in place."

Kirk realized that Oathmeyer was almost certainly referring to Francois and his organization.

Frank and Kirk would be going to Pigeon Forge, Tennessee, where they would establish separate residences near the Mountain Rapids Motel, which was a small motel located on the Pigeon River and was ostensibly owned by an American investment group.

"I caution you both that your presence in the Smokies will be primarily to remain in the area in the event your talents are required," Lennie stated. "We are almost certain that the motel is actually owned, or at least managed, by Ali Salim Bakara, an Afghani male who lives at the motel and who apparently has led a somewhat sedate lifestyle for the last twenty-two years in the Smoky Mountain region.

"From a pattern involving phone calls following the operation in Paris, analysts strongly felt that Ali was the key individual receiving information, rather than someone relaying it on to higher echelons. If this turns out to be the case, we have a "Mr. Big" living in an area where irreparable harm could be done."

After several hours of discussion, Kirk and Frank were aware that their assignment would almost completely involve hanging out in the area and waiting for orders. They would not openly socialize and would maintain contact only through secure cellular phones.

Because the assignment originated as a domestic investigation, Lenny wanted to ensure that his personnel were involved in a lower profile aspect of the operation. "It behooves us to have the bureau run the lead on this one," Oathmeyer stated. "If there are fireworks, then we want to make sure they're the ones who light the match."

"Sounds like the old plausible deniability approach," thought Frank.

Following the meeting with their supervisor, Kirk and Frank returned to their respective offices, where they would begin the preliminary work of establishing a cover story for their proposed travel to Tennessee, generating suitable identification, and developing a workable background that would ensure neither of the spies would be suspected by those they might encounter during the assignment.

Frank Gale had somewhat of a head start because he'd been born just thirty-five miles away, in Knoxville, and as a child he had spent countless summer days in the mountainous area.

Kirk accessed a website from the city of Pigeon Forge, Tennessee, and began learning the history of the area, community calendar, special events, maps, and related information that might assist in his assignment.

As the two conducted their own research, federal agents from other intelligence groups pursued searches that would yield the same results.

The workload of the two operatives was reduced to an extent when Leonard Oathmeyer brought in two thick folders that provided somewhat dated but valuable files on the background of Ali Salim Bakara and his journey to his new country.

Kirk decided that his cover name would be Alex A. Strait. As his research continued, he found that a suitable place for short-term lodging was at the Cold Creek Resort on the parkway in Pigeon Forge. This location was within walking distance of Mountain Rapids motel and was also next door to a Bojangles Carryout, where he could be ensured of regular, if not healthy, food and snacks.

After calling and making reservations at Cold Creek, Kurt walked into the adjoining supply area where he issued himself a Tennessee driver's license, a bank card, and a Tennessee concealed weapons permit. Kirk was aware that within a half hour, these documents would reflect that they had been issued by the necessary offices within the State of Tennessee. He would also rent a car when he arrived at the airport in Alcoa, Tennessee, that would display registration plates for that state.

Kirk spent the remainder of his day reviewing surveillance tapes and virtual reality mapping of the Mountain Rapids complex. He noted that the time stamp on the video documentation had started on the previous day, a sure indication that someone else was already on the job.

After finishing his tasks, Kirk left the office to return to his government-supplied apartment at Watergate. After having a frozen lasagna, his mind began a turn by turn tour of the life on which he had embarked. He wondered if his dad would have understood his chosen profession—and more important, would he have appreciated the fact that his son was to a large degree the catalyst that had gotten his father's assailant killed? The answer wouldn't come.

Perhaps the biggest area of concern to Kirk was that although he had no compulsions about taking the life of Masoud Ali Al-Wakim during an event similar to combat conditions, he remained uncomfortable when reliving the death of his first victim in Colorado, David Franklin Lowe. Kirk questioned himself on the morality of the hit but eventually decided it was time to change his trend of thought.

"Kill as directed and let God, or Allah, sort them out," he reasoned.

Chapter 41

Shortly after five o'clock the following morning, Kirk was awakened by the incessant ringing of his telephone. The call was from Lennie Oathmeyer, who used a tone of voice that Kirk had not heard before.

"Kirk, get to the office ten minutes ago. We have a crisis," he stated.

"I'm on the way," Kirk replied, and he immediately began an expedited routine of dressing for work.

Forty-five minutes later, Kirk entered the private entrance at the Bureau of Prisons and was promptly summoned into Lennie's office.

"This is going to be a hard pill to swallow, son," Lennie said. "Last evening, Nur began her assignment in Paris. Her job was to retrace the steps the two of you and made and to identify any discernable changes in the pattern of the neighborhood. I had her under discreet surveillance by one of my other operatives who, for obvious security reasons, maintained a loose tail on her. It appears that the third time she entered the area; a street vendor approached, detained, and escorted her to a small home two blocks from her encounter. Nur was wearing the traditional prayer outfit and was facially covered," Lennie added. "An emergency transponder in a cell phone that was taped to her leg was activated within two minutes of the abduction. NSA has the grid coordinates of the emergency transponder, and because it is still active, we can only assume the signal has not been discovered. We can only presume that Nur has not provided any information other than her cover story and that the enemy hasn't yet resorted to any type of torture."

It was at this moment that Frank Gale entered after receiving a similar call instructing him to report to the office. Lennie noted his watch at the moment that Frank walked through the door.

"Frank, there's been a change of plans, and I don't have the time to provide a full briefing to you," Lennie stated. "Kirk will brief you, but as of now, you'll be reporting to the Tennessee assignment alone. Have you prepared your cover and preparatory research?"

"I was going to finish it this morning," Frank stated.

"Kirk, have you finished yours?" Oathmeyer asked.

"Yes, I was ready to travel."

"Transfer your paperwork, rework the identity for Frank, and then prepare to leave immediately for Paris," Oathmeyer ordered. "When you two have worked out the plans, review with me, and then Kirk will leave for Paris, and Frank will get to the Smoky Mountains."

A half hour later, Frank Gale had become Alex Strait. Lennie was satisfied with the quick response and dispatched Frank to head for the mountains.

"Kirk, issue yourself a new identity under the name of Wiley A. Groat on your diplomatic passport, prepare associated paperwork, and plan on leaving Dulles at 6:12 p.m. on Flight 1284 to Orly," he stated. "Lois will have your ticket prepared in the Groat name, and it will be ready at the ticket counter when you get to Dulles. You will be a US State Department courier with diplomatic status, and you will be authorized to carry a classified courier bag that will not be inspected by US or French customs. Take disguises and weapons inside your courier kit."

Kirk immediately began his preparations and by noon was back at his condo packing his bags for Paris. He was now Wiley A. Groat, a state department diplomat whose diplomatic passport ensured that he was entitled to the utmost professional courtesy in any country.

"Enjoy your flight," stated the attractive flight attendant as she escorted Mr. Groat to his first-class seat.

Chapter 42

Throughout the day and during his flight, Kirk had received countless secure text messages from Lois Harding. Upon arrival at Orly International Airport in Paris, he would be met by Francois, whose assistance during the previous assignment had been invaluable. Francois would coordinate a meeting between Kirk and another American, "Mr. Broom." A detailed briefing from Broom would be forthcoming when the two hooked up in Paris.

Perhaps the most interesting text of the day from Lois sent revealed a clue to the severity of the situation in which Kirk was involved. The NSA had intercepted a cryptic message from a home on Rue de la Roquette in Paris to Ali Salim Bakara at the Mountain Rapids Motel in Tennessee. The message indicated, "A person of interest is being detained regarding the recent unfortunate incident in Paris."

Kirk began wondering most chillingly, "Is it possible that Al Qaeda is operating from a headquarters *within* the United States?"

Chapter 43

Francois was waiting at the arrival gate, and Kirk followed him to the parking garage where a driver smoking a cigarette stood next to a small van casually.

"Your counterpart, a Mr. Broom, has maintained constant surveillance on the house since the incident occurred," stated Francois. "We have an assistant with him. They have adequate arms and supplies, and both have the utmost experience in rescue operations. Certain heat-seeking devices that have been utilized in monitoring the house show that one individual has remained in a location in the back bedroom the entire time. We are convinced this is your missing operative, and thankfully she is still alive, as evidenced by her body heat signature."

Kirk learned that normally three individuals were inside the residence with the hostage. One individual would usually remain inside the bedroom, and every two hours the terrorists would rotate their positions within the home.

Chapter 44

Nur Jasmin now knew something she wished she had learned through surveillance of the Parisian neighborhood, rather than learning firsthand through her captors. Women wearing their covered prayer outfits, would open and close their hand at certain strategic locations while traversing the area. Had she realized this in the first place, she would not now be bound and shackled inside the confines of a small bedroom facing a menacing Iranian who wielded an AK 47 automatic rifle.

She was aware that thus far her cover story had not been shredded—otherwise she would not be alive. Apparently her assailants were waiting for orders on how to proceed. Despite extensive questioning, she had maintained her story of survival following the death of her husband, a martyr who had received his reward from Allah when he perished after igniting an explosive backpack in a tea house in Yemeni—an act that, by the way, had killed two American tourists.

Her story was one that, if true, merited respect from her abductors. Thus she remained yet to be thoroughly searched or physically mistreated—or else a life-saving GPS phone and a 9mm Glock taped to her legs would have been discovered. Nur knew that her time was quickly running out. With her hands bound behind her by plastic restraining bands, there was no chance of accessing her weapon or calling for help. She could only pray to a divine, compassionate Allah that he would smile with benevolence on her life-threatening situation.

She also prayed that her brothers and sisters in the global fight against terrorism were aware of her situation and location and would, at any moment, break through the door to rescue her.

Nur shed silent tears as she continued to reflect on her situation.

Chapter 45

Kirk and Francois got out of their vehicle a block from the targeted residence on Rue de la Roquette. They surreptitiously climbed a fire escape and crossed several adjoining roofs, where Kirk met two shadowy figures concealed in a small corner and surrounded by binoculars, night vision scopes, high-powered sniper rifles, and concussion grenades. Kirk could not recall seeing this amount of military equipment since attending a weapons assembly arms room at Fort Rucker, Alabama.

"I'm Wiley Groat," stated the traveling diplomat as he extended his hand to Leslie McCarter.

"Pleased to formally meet you, Kirk," replied McCarter. "I've witnessed some of your work and appreciate your dedication and ability." The Broom inwardly enjoyed the opportunity to inform his counterpart that he was aware of his true identity.

The irony was not overlooked by Kirk. He then met The Broom's associate, Pierre, an agency counterpart from the Legion. The two shook hands.

While maintaining a vigil on the target home directly across the street, McCarter began briefing Kirk. "I haven't left this site since our asset was abducted. She remains in possession of a concealed phone—which, by the way, can be utilized as an open communication to transmit when accessed by our stateside operations. I receive regular updates on the contents of the questioning. However, her cellular expends more battery use when we're on open transmit, and we're trying to save the hundred-hour battery life for as long as we can. At this time, we have a battery life of approximately ten more hours. Our goal will be to rescue her before either the phone or she is dead."

Kirk also learned of the cover story that Nur had relayed to her captors and that was monitored by the NSA Electronic Surveillance Program. He marveled at the ingenuity of the contents. Even the most hardened of terrorists would be reluctant to end the life of someone who had been so close to the martyr she had described as her late husband.

Leslie McCarter was obviously the on-scene commander and would make the operational rules of rescue. Kirk was again a soldier, ready to serve his country in whatever role was assigned. "What operational plans have you developed Leslie?" asked Kirk.

McCarter thought for a full thirty seconds before responding to the question. "At 5:15 a.m., the changing of the guard will take place. At 5:05 a.m., we're going through that door. We will terminate three Iranian cockroaches and will be placing a very much alive hostage into a van that pulls to the front door at the exact moment we remove the door with plastique explosives. There will be no enemy prisoners taken, and our own agents will be safely extracted." Leslie McCarter made one last statement that made Kirk Alexander proud to serve the country he loved so much. "Just as in Viet Nam, we will not leave any of our soldiers or allies behind, and that's an order."

For the next several hours the assault team rested while discussing and formulating plans for the pending incursion into the terrorist safe house. Kirk marveled at the efficiency of Leslie McCarter as he contacted operational associates within NSA and provided instructions. At exactly 5:03 a.m., NSA would activate the vibrating mode on the cellular phone that was taped to Nur's leg. This would be her alert to be prepared to remain in a fixed location until her rescuers reached her.

It was further decided that McCarter, having extensive experience in the use of explosives, would plant the explosive on the front door of the residence and, upon removing the door, would be the first rescuer in. He would be followed by Kirk, who would be the first combatant to enter the room where Nur was being held.

Francois would be the third rescuer through the door and would possess a 9mm British Sterling machine gun for cleanup work.

"When Kirk reaches our asset, he will not worry at that time about removing her bonds but will carry her to the van," McCarter stated. "Kirk, you will yell clear when you have our hostage and are leaving the bedroom. Francois will follow you and our hostage. I will be the last one out of the residence."

Pierre would drive the van to the front door of the residence two seconds after the plastique explosion. All combatants entering the home would wear bullet-resistant vests and Kevlar helmets, and they would possess concussion grenades that could disorientate the enemy. "Pierre, upon arrival at the front door, you will exit the vehicle, open the side cargo door, and then immediately return to the driver seat for immediate departure when all four of us are inside," McCarter ordered.

The hostage extraction team had just over one hour until green light time—the moment of rescue or death.

The final hour was spent in gathering equipment that had been utilized during the days of surveillance and packing the contents that would no longer be required for the operation. These items were carefully placed in a jump bag, a canvas container that Pierre would return to the van prior to the assault. Each of the combatants donned their equipment and, through a buddy system of support, inspected and made adjustments to the military arsenal that each of them donned. Although each of the soldiers was wearing camouflage, ironically they were uniforms of the elite Iranian Revolutionary Guard.

At 4:50 a.m., Pierre retrieved the jump bag and departed for the van, which was parked a block away. He would drive onto Rue de la Roquette and wait with lights out until he saw the assault personnel crossing the street. Then, two seconds after the explosion, he would race to the front door to complete his tasks.

McCarter gave hand signals to the members of his team. They made a quick inspection of the area to ensure there was no trace of their presence on the roof. The Broom led his team down a rear fire escape, where they walked through a small alley between buildings and faced the doorway of the targeted residence, just forty feet away.

At exactly 5:03 a.m., Nur Jasmin was awakened as her vibrating cellular phone alerted her from an already restless sleep. She noted that her guard was asleep in a chair that faced the couch on which she was lying. He held his AK 47 across his lap.

Nur realized that this was a signal that rescuers were on the way. She didn't move when the vibrator stirred her for the second time. She began formulating her own plan of action. "At all costs I must stay low and out of the line of fire, and wait for help," she thought.

Chapter 46

These were the moments that Leslie McCarter lived for. He was a career soldier who loved his country and the opportunities he had found in life to make it a better place to live. There was no fear in his heart.

McCarter monitored his watch ticking off seconds as his team stood crouched in the small alley. At exactly 5:05 a.m. he motioned with his right hand, and the team, crouched almost to the ground, ran silently across the avenue. McCarter affixed the plastique door opener to the wood frame, his team huddled against the wall, and then The Broom clicked a detonator.

The sound and concussion were terrific for those who were expecting it—and almost catastrophic for those inside. Fragments of the doorway were still airborne as McCarter entered and shot a captor in the forehead as he began to rise from a couch. He moved further inside the door to allow his team room for entering.

Kirk ran to the right of McCarter and approached the closed bedroom door where Nur was believed to be confined.

Nur was stunned by the tremendous explosion from the front of the house but was fully cognizant that rescuers were on the way. She was amazed that her captor was responding so quickly and realized that he was already on his feet and pointing his weapon toward the door. She knew that the first person through the door would surely take the full blast from the Russian-manufactured weapon.

Although her hands were bound behind her, Nur sprang from the couch where she had been confined and dove into the back of her assailant. As the door of the bedroom opened, the assailant was falling into the wall. Nur could hear the machine gun firing into the ceiling as she attempted to roll away from the firefight that was about to ensue.

Kirk came through the door like a speeding train. He immediately fired two bullets from his Glock into the head of Nur's captor while the terrorist's AK-47 continued to spray the room and walls.

Almost immediately Nur found herself being picked up and thrown over the shoulder of her rescuer. As Kirk yelled clear while carrying her from the room, Leslie McCarter glanced in his direction. Kirk looked in the direction of Leslie, quickly raised his right hand, and fired yet another shot. McCarter could feel the percussion as the bullet passed his head. He looked to his left and realized that a terrorist had come from another room and was in the process of pointing a weapon at Leslie; Kirk's quick actions had just saved his life.

Kirk ran from the house and deposited his friend on the back seat of the vehicle. He was quickly followed by Francois, who entered the van yet remained poised to return to retrieve McCarter if necessary.

McCarter ran from the door of the residence, stopped, and threw a canvas satchel through the hole that had previously been the front door. He dove into the cargo door of the van while yelling, "Go, go, go!"

The van was fifty yards from the terrorist home when the entire building burst into a wall of flames and flying debris.

"I owe you one, soldier," said McCarter to Kirk as the van expedited from the scene.

"We both owe her one, soldier," replied Kirk while nodding toward Nur. "She attacked a combatant from the rear and saved me from being another body filled with lead."

"Hoo-rah," was Leslie McCarter's only response.

Chapter 47

Within two minutes of the successful rescue, Leslie McCarter had notified Leonard Oathmeyer of the outcome. Lennie immediately called Senator Wingate, who at this very moment was briefing the president of the United States.

Because the American team, Nur, Kirk, and McCarter, were going straight to Orly International Airport where a flight chartered by the US State Department was waiting, the team spent their travel time congratulating each other on a job well done.

Although McCarter knew that an immediate debriefing of the hostage was necessary for operational and intelligence purposes, he elected not to begin this process while in front of the French intelligence personnel. He chose to wait until he, Nur, and Kirk were on their plane.

Privately, McCarter was concerned that he had narrowly missed death because Francois, who was in a key position to protect his flank, had failed in that aspect of the mission. Thanks to Kirk, McCarter was still alive, and in turn, thanks to Nur Jasmin, both he and Kirk would see another sunrise.

"I'll let the brain trust of Langley sort through the details, and they can release intelligence as they see fit," thought Leslie. "The devil is always in the details."

Upon arriving at the waiting flight, all baggage was transferred into the passenger area of the plane, there were a series of hugs and high fives, and the weary team entered the sanctity of a US plane where, in under eight hours, they would land at Andrews Air Force Base in Maryland.

French intelligence at the request of U.S. agents had retrieved Nur's belongings from her hotel following her abduction.

Chapter 48

While debriefing Nur during the initial stages of the flight, McCarter and Kirk realized that Nur's survival and ability to avoid torture—or worse—were based on two significant items. First, her cover story relating to the sacred sacrifice by her martyred husband had bought her time. Secondly, when Masoud Ali Al-Wakim had been terminated with prejudice by Nur and Kirk on their previous trip to Paris, that death had left a void in leadership that hadn't been filled. In short, the Iranian hostage takers had known what was expected of them and had done their jobs well. But due to a leadership void, they had no immediate contact with anyone who would instruct them how to proceed in interrogating their captive.

McCarter contacted Lennie Oathmeyer with his immediate briefing after instructing his team to shower, get some much needed rest, and change into clothing that would be more appropriate upon arrival at Andrews.

The team would be able to get four hours of needed sleep as their flight continued to the waiting arms of the United States of America.

Chapter 49

Senator Royal T. Wingate stood next to his operations director, Leonard Oathmeyer, as the passengers walked from the plane. Oathmeyer quickly introduced the three operatives to the senator and explained to Wingate the roles that each had played in the Paris operation.

"The president of the United States, on behalf of a grateful nation, including me, thank you for your performance of duty in safeguarding our citizens," the senator stated. He shook each of the agents' hands and immediately turned to enter his chauffeured Lincoln Town Car for his return to Capitol Hill.

"Get a good night of rest and meet me in the office at 8:30 a.m.," Oathmeyer stated to his team as he too entered the senator's car.

Three separate vans with tinted windows would take each team member to their respective residences where sleep would come easily and peacefully.

As McCarter rode from the main gate of Andrews Air Force Base onto Suitland Parkway, his cellular rang.

"Broom, this is Oathmeyer. I'd appreciate it if you could be a bit earlier in the morning, let's say about 7:30."

"I'll be there, Chief," replied McCarter.

McCarter was only too well aware that being summoned into an office where he rarely went was quite a deviation from the established normalcy that had existed for several years. The one thing McCarter knew more than anything was the fact that he was a soldier who would follow all orders of his commander.

Chapter 50

The Broom lived life with a philosophy that if he wasn't at least fifteen minutes early for a meeting, this meant he was an hour late. He arrived at the offices of the Bureau of Prisons at 7:15 a.m. and met Lennie Oathmeyer as he was opening the door. Lois Harding was already at her desk and poured coffee for the two as they entered.

Lennie didn't waste time and began asking questions that he would in turn relay to key members of the intelligence community within a matter of hours.

"Kirk Alexander is as good as anyone I've seen," McCarter reported. "He doesn't question direction, follows orders, and is at the top of his game. Pierre, the driver, performed flawlessly. He's a credit to the French.

"I've previously briefed you on Francois," McCarter stated. "He almost got us all killed, and that is a sin I consider unforgivable. Nur, the hostage, I'm holding reservations on. She should have been more proactive in her surveillance operations, and then we never would have had to face this issue. Quite frankly, Lennie, from my vantage point a block away, I picked up on the hand signals that were given by the women as they traversed the area. Nur should have shown more in security awareness."

Leonard Oathmeyer leaned back in his chair, crossed his arms over his chest, closed his eyes, and then nodded affirmatively. "I see some problems I need to correct," he stated simply.

At 8:20 a.m., Kirk entered the office followed a few minutes later by Nur Jasmin. Lois provided coffee, and the three agents sat with Lennie as they further discussed the most recent operation. Lennie obviously did not reflect on the conversation that had previously been held between him and McCarter.

After an hour, Leonard Oathmeyer advised he was due for a meeting on Capitol Hill. "You know the drill, kiddies, he stated. "Get those after-action reports in the works. We have a nonstop schedule coming our way."

For the next three days, employees of the BOP office of Central Intelligence would write reports to be debriefed, analyzed, and psychoanalyzed, and the final report would be sent to Oathmeyer, where he would determine remedial action, guidance, or restore his operatives to full duty.

Leonard Oathmeyer would keep the comments made regarding Nur's activities in the file cabinet of his mind.

Chapter 51

Following his meeting with Senator Wingate, Leonard Oathmeyer had gone to the NSA Headquarters at Fort Meade, Maryland, where he was now seated with his colleagues—Matthew Hellerman, director of Central Intelligence; Frank G. Sanders, director of the Federal Bureau of Investigation; and Admiral Thurmont Delia, director of the National Security Administration.

The attorney general and the secretary of state were noticeably absent from the meeting. In an effort to explain the absence of these key government employees, CIA Director Hellerman simply stated, "This is one of those times when plausible deniability comes into the game of war, thanks in great part to former President of the U.S., Richard M. Nixon."

Each of the agencies currently had their own operatives in place in the Smoky Mountain area, working independently yet performing their tasks based on strategies that originated at meetings such as this. There had been numerous meetings in the past few days.

"We currently have communication intercepts monitoring the motel in Pigeon Forge. All phones and text messages of all players we're currently aware of are being monitored. As I understand it, continual satellite imagery of the motel is also active," stated Sanders of the FBI.

Admiral Delia of NSA confirmed the satellite operations that were producing imagery of all traffic entering or departing the motel.

Leonard Oathmeyer advised the team that he had personnel in the area who were fully prepared for any type of dirty work that may be required.

All present nodded in complete agreement, and the meeting continued with more precise planning in the event that a preemptive strike may be needed in the foreseeable future against the suspected operation in the Smokies.

One of the most perplexing matters that had not been resolved was the fact that since the rescue operation in Paris, no one was known to have made contact with Ali Salim Bakara at the Mountain Rapids Motel in Pigeon Forge, Tennessee. The cryptic message, indicating a person of interest was being detained, had been the only reference to the unfolding events.

"Gentlemen," stated Admiral Thurmont Delia of the NSA, "I need to remind us all that the Oak Ridge National Laboratory, the home of the 1943 Manhattan Project where we pioneered a method to produce and separate plutonium, is just an hour away from Pigeon Forge. "As you all know, it remains a top secret complex that is indispensable to the US Department of Energy, and an attack at ORNL could be a catastrophe unlike anything the world has ever witnessed, including Hiroshima."

There was not an abundance of enthusiasm as the meeting was adjourned for this session.

Chapter 52

Frank G. Sanders, the director of the Federal Bureau of Investigation, fully realized the pressure he was under on a daily basis. In view of the fact that the FBI was performing its investigation in a lead role in Tennessee, Sanders could feel the heat from bureaucrats inside other agencies who were monitoring every move his department made.

Sanders had begun his career as a young police officer in Miami Beach, Florida, and had attended college during his off duty hours. Hard work and tenacity had led him to a degree in criminal justice, a subsequent law degree, and a fast track course that, at the age of fifty-seven, had landed him an appointment as director of what had become one of the premier investigative agencies in the federal government.

Despite everything he had learned in life, Sanders remained steadfast in the simplicity of his logic. He believed that every investigation he was involved in or reviewed needed to show the elements of who, what, when, where, and why.

The director had returned to his office following the meeting at Fort Meade and was surrounded by key individuals of his staff, including analyst, investigators, profilers, high echelon command, and legal personnel. They were searching for the answers, and Sanders had added a new equation to those questions: to what extent could the country be harmed?

In opening his meeting, Director Sanders asked a senior analyst, Greg Wilson, to provide an overview of counter terrorist operations that the director knew would set a theme and flavor for the meeting and objectives. Sanders had listened to Wilson on numerous occasions in the past and was fully cognizant that his analyst had the intelligence, knowledge, and patriotism to influence and further motivate his team.

Greg Wilson, a straight-talking, no-nonsense, career federal employee, had long since left diplomacy in a former office. He would say what needed to be said when asked to comment.

"Thank you, Director Sanders," Wilson stated as he stood up while nodding to the gathered team.

"Gentlemen, in 1984, the Reagan administration referred to a war on terror. Later, former President Bush called our current situation a war on terror. The current president prefers to use the term 'overseas contingency operations.' In my own humble opinion, I just prefer to call our situation World War III, a war that is international in focus yet now is being fought on the very lands that our forefathers fought for, just so they could live away from tyranny and threat from others.

"There was a simpler time when terrorists were poor and considered themselves crusaders. Now, we find ourselves fighting a larger group: the crusaders, the crazies, and the criminals. They're no longer poor, yet they have sponsorship of elements in society who possess the funding, have access to the weaponry, and are fanatically obsessed with the destruction of our people, country, and way of life.

"I'm not here to teach history, but to provide facts. September 2000: The USS *Cole* was bombed while in a foreign port. September 11, 2001: attacks on the World Trade Center, the Pentagon, and In 2003, there was a plot to blow up the Brooklyn Bridge.

"I won't dwell on it, except to remind us all not to overlook the targeting of the International Monetary Fund Buildings, Columbus Shopping Mall Bombing Plot, Fort Dix attack plot, and others," Wilson softly added, and then he continued. "President George W. Bush defined objectives in the war on terror. Defeat terrorists such as Osama Bin Laden and Abu Musab al-Zarqawi, and destroy their organizations. For the record, al-Zarqawi was killed during an air strike by US forces on June 7, 2006, near Baghdad."

Wilson continued with his message following that footnote. "Identify, locate, and destroy terrorists along with their organizations. End the state sponsorship of terrorism. Interdict and disrupt material support for terrorists. Eliminate terrorist sanctuaries and havens. Defend US citizens and interests at home and abroad. Attain domain awareness."

Greg Wilson nodded again at the FBI director and took his seat. Sanders only had one question to ask his outspoken assistant.

"Greg, what are your personal feelings regarding the ongoing investigation in Tennessee?" he asked.

There was no hesitation with Wilson's candid answer. "These Islamic extremists are hell-bent on getting to heaven so that Allah can reward them with those seven virgins. I think we should expedite their journey while they're still young enough to know what a virgin is," he answered.

As the meeting was finished, Director Frank Sanders asked Greg to remain for a minute.

"Any immediate thoughts?" Sanders asked.

"Just one, sir," Greg said. "I mentioned earlier about interdicting and disrupting the enemy. Well, if someone were inspecting a facility in the hospitality industry, couldn't they find problems and then put pressure on them to find a new maintenance engineer, or be shut down?"

Sounds like a great assignment for the deep covers who deal with the dirty stuff," Wilson noted as he walked from the room.

Ten minutes later, Leonard Oathmeyer and Frank Sanders had developed their own little plan that could be phased in without a need to consult anyone higher than Senator Wingate.

"Damn, that's a great idea, boy," replied the senator. "Go for it!"

Chapter 53

Following his own meeting with his counterparts in the intelligence community, Leonard Oathmeyer had returned to his office at the Bureau of Prisons where a fifty-two-page report on the hostage extraction, statements of his agents, and intelligence reports and recommendations awaited his final review.

Page seventeen of the lengthy report left Oathmeyer in a major conundrum. At one point during her captivity, the covered headdress worn by Nur Jasmin had been removed, and photographs of her face had been obtained by the enemy.

Lennie fully realized that unless those photographs had been destroyed during the rescue and subsequent explosion, members of Al Qaeda almost certainly had pictures of one of his agents, which in the future could compromise her own safety or the security of anyone seen with her.

Oathmeyer immediately contacted Senator Wingate and briefed him with this most disturbing information. The matter was discussed for a full ten minutes before Lennie hung up the phone and instructed Lois Harding to locate Nur and have her report to his office immediately. "Tell Nur to wear a covered prayer outfit when she comes," advised Lennie. The last thing Leonard Oathmeyer wanted was for an enemy operative to recognize Nur Jasmin and to follow her to an office where deep undercover personnel were assigned.

Chapter 54

An hour later, Nur Jasmin sat with her employer as they discussed her captivity in-depth. Nur understood the reasons for concern and was in complete agreement with the associative dangers she could place on other personnel as well as a threat that could now be directed at her.

"Mr. Oathmeyer, I love my job, and more than that, I love this country," Nur stated. "What are my options in this matter?"

In view of the fact that the enemy had neglected to take fingerprints of Nur, there remained possibilities that would ensure her continued value to the government of her adoptive country.

"Option one," stated Lennie, "would be a transfer to FBI, NSA, or the Department of State, where you would be utilized in translating documents and intelligence from Farsi or Arabic.

"Option two would be complete facial reconstruction that would, as I understand it, end with a new facial identity, and if successful, it would bring you back to this office in seven to eight months where, after a bit of retraining, you'd return to your covert status."

In the mind of Nur Jasmin, there was only one option.

"Develop a new cover story and generate suitable identification, and Lois will make the necessary arrangements for travel to one of our medical facilities in Rhode Island," Lennie said.

Nur left the office an hour later, confident that all expenses would be compensated by Uncle Sam.

"This is truly a great country," thought Nur as she returned to her apartment to pack for an extended absence from the work she loved to perform.

Chapter 55

Frank Gale, under the alias of Alex Strait, had settled in at the Cold Creek Resort quickly. His first several days had involved learning his way around the area of Pigeon Forge and Gatlinburg, and during the evening he would spend quality time at the Texas Roadhouse Restaurant on the Parkway in Pigeon Forge. While eating the ribs that would almost dissolve in his mouth, he allowed himself to exceed his per diem allotment on a daily basis, just to enjoy his dinner.

"I know how much I have, but don't know how long I have to spend it," the agent thought with an inward smile.

Melissa, the bartender, had seemed somewhat disappointed when she had learned he was not related to the country entertainer, George Strait.

Frank had on one occasion walked into Bojangles Carryout and recognized a face from his earlier career as an FBI agent. He and the other agent had briefly met during a situational awareness seminar at Quantico, Virginia. They completely ignored each other while facing each other from separate tables.

The sheer number of tourists in the area provided anonymity to the dozens of new faces who were covertly tracking several targets to and from the Mountain Rapids Motel.

Frank was jogging when his cellular phone began vibrating. He noted from the caller ID that it was from a restricted number. He stopped because this was always a call he had to take.

"Frank," stated Lennie Oathmeyer, "I've got a little task that's exactly what you've always wanted to do."

"I'm always up to a new challenge, Lennie."

Lennie Oathmeyer went on to explain that the management of the

Mountain Rapids Motel was going to be inspected by the Sevier County Health Department and that numerous discrepancies would be found.

"Wear some old clothes tomorrow and redneck yourself up a bit more, if that's possible," Lennie said. "You may need to apply for a motel maintenance position."

Chapter 56

Scarcely an hour later, Ali Salim Bakara was approached by a representative of the local health department concerning their semiannual on-site health and safety inspection. Bakara wasn't concerned because he personally performed all repairs that were needed at the motel.

Close to an hour later, the inspector, identified as Roger Fleming, displayed his complete list of twenty-eight deficiencies, five which were safety related and would necessitate an immediate closing of the motel until the facility was in compliance with county and state law.

"Who handles your maintenance here, Alley?" asked the code officer.

"The name is *Ali,*" Bakara replied, "and I handle all of the work."

"It's a shame my nephew doesn't work here," Fleming replied. "He's a real whiz at getting places back in mechanical order and up to code."

The hook had been taken by the fish, and the fish was on the line. Reeling him in was just a matter of agreeing to give a new maintenance man a couple of days to correct the major issues instead of immediately closing the business.

Ali Salim Bakara was seething after being assured that Mr. Fleming's nephew, Alex, would be at the motel the following day at 9:00 a.m. to discuss employment and assist Bakara in remaining open to a most appreciative tourist economy.

When contacted by Lennie Oathmeyer, Frank advised he would accept the position if offered, even though he didn't like working for minimum wage.

"Not to worry son," replied Oathmeyer. "You're going to save a lot of money while earning it at minimum wage, rather than spending your per diem on Texas Roadhouse beers.

Frank wondered if there was any end to the knowledge Oathmeyer possessed, even when his personnel were deep undercover and seemingly not accounted for.

Chapter 57

The following morning, Frank drove into the parking lot of the Mountain Rapids Motel and approached Ali Salim Bakara, who stood behind the counter in the office.

Bakara had resigned himself to the fact that for his motel to remain open for the immediate future, he would probably be forced to hire this relative of a code enforcement inspector. Although Bakara had usually been the recipient of bribes during favor exchanges, he was also wise to the ways of the Middle East as well as the ways of his adoptive country. Business was business.

Despite the circumstances surrounding his presence, Frank was personable enough, treated his potential employer with respect, and was willing to accept minimal wage. He completed a one-page application that asked for not much more than a name, address, and social security number.

The only reference that Frank put on his employment application was the name of Roger Fleming of the Sevier County Health Department. One reference was all that Bakara needed, yet it was one that he would make every effort not to contact.

"My uncle is more interested in me working than I am," stated Frank. "I think he just wants to see me out of my mother's hair.

"Good news," thought Bakara. "He may just want to work for enough time for the local government to forget I exist."

The employment interview was so simple that within ten minutes Bakara gave the inspection list to Alex with the simple instructions, "Fix these."

Both Leonard Oathmeyer and FBI Director Sanders would bask in the intelligence community limelight when certain department heads became aware that the two had been instrumental in placing an undercover investigator inside the middle of the operation.

Within two days, Frank had strategically placed assorted intercept equipment, concealed cameras, and one major item of interest inside the confines of the motel.

Admiral Thurmont Delia was most impressed with the new sources of intelligence that originated from within the motel, thanks to the additions and installations that the new maintenance man was able to "fix."

Chapter 58

Ali Bakara had been born in Afghanistan in 1950. He considered himself a devout Muslim, although in actuality he spent more time thinking about money than Allah. He had married at the age of twenty and, as many potential terrorists, had concentrated in the field of social work.

In the early 1980s, Ali was introduced to Osama Bin Laden, who had been recruited by the US government to fight against the Russians in the mountains of Afghanistan and Pakistan. It had been Osama who encouraged a young Bakara to further his education in the United States. This was a sentiment that Bakara had held for some time, and thanks to encouragement from someone he respected, he decided to take that advice.

In the months of preparing endless requests to further his education in America, Osama had the opportunity to share more of his inner feelings, and some suggestions, to Bakara.

"You can live a good life in that country, but never forget where you came from; never trust a Russian or like an American, but take whatever handout they are willing to provide.

Following his attendance and additional education from the University of Georgia, Ali Salim Bakara moved his family to the area of the Smoky Mountains. Although he hated all the trees, he did feel closer to home with the surrounding mountains.

Later, one of Osama Bin Laden's associates stopped by Bakara's home in Pigeon Forge, Tennessee, one afternoon, expressed the best wishes of Bin Laden, and gave Bakara a paper bag filled with US currency. "He is hopeful you will purchase a motel so that on occasion, when our countrymen visit, they will have a friendly face with adequate lodging."

Osama Bin Laden had also instructed his emissary to share a passage from the Koran: "Slay the pagos wherever ye find them."

A month later, Bakara purchased the Mountain Rapids Motel, a Mecca for those who traveled.

Ali had not heard from Osama Bin Laden again until the year 2000. Mohamed Atta, an Egyptian guest and a flight student attending training in the United States, needed a place to rest and meet with some long time friends in a friendly and private atmosphere. Bakara was only too happy to share his success and hospitality.

Despite the fact that the US government had some files on Bakara, he was an enigma. Intelligence was old dated, and with the exception of recent phone and computer chatter, he had for too many years remained under an umbrella of secrecy.

Perhaps Lennie Oathmeyer had expressed his thoughts adequately to Senator Royal T. Wingate. "We just need to investigate the problem, evaluate the problem, isolate the problem, and then eliminate the other problems that surface," Oathmeyer stated.

There had never been a doubt in the mind of Leonard Oathmeyer that as long as he had the support, he had the personnel who would reduce the dangers of the world to an acceptable level.

Chapter 59

Although Ali Salim Bakara had been angry when presented with the option of hiring Alex Strait to perform maintenance at his motel, he was slowly seeing the benefits of his coerced decision.

Alex obviously had contacts that could access equipment and fixtures that needed to be installed in correcting the code enforcement problems that had been identified. And because he had contacts, Alex was able to obtain much of the equipment free, from friends who owed him favors. Ali was delighted that his new employee needed little direction or supervision, spent limited time inside the office, and reported to work without the smell of moonshine on his breath. Even the new smoke detectors that had been installed reflected the quality that was only found in better products.

Unknown to Bakara, these quality smoke detectors were providing outstanding color video and sound to a small monitoring post inside a motel room just a block from Mountain Rapids. One of the smoke detectors was inside room 111, the suite that had been designated by Ali Salim Bakara as the VIP room for important guests.

Roger Fleming of the Sevier County Code Enforcement Office had contacted Bakara by phone to ensure repairs were being conducted quickly and efficiently. "I sure can't close you down at a time when you're working so hard to ensure the safety of our tourists," Fleming had stated.

Ali Bakara at one time had been a creature of suspicion. His years in Afghanistan had trained him to be cognizant of his surroundings and to see potential problems and avoid them. Unfortunately, the good life as a motel owner had dulled some of his capabilities; Ali was more suspicious of receiving a counterfeit piece of currency than identifying counterfeit people who on a daily basis were repairing street lights, maintaining ongoing road construction projects, or working on-site to improve the efficiency of his business.

Frank, on the other hand, remained at the top of his game. Whenever Ali Salim Bakara would check to ensure his employee was working, Frank would be heavily engrossed in his tasks. He carried a pager that would be activated by a surveillance team for an alert that Ali was prowling the grounds.

Because of the alertness of Frank, leadership in the intelligence community was also aware of a photograph that was carefully hung on the wall of Bakara's private office and displayed a young man of apparent Middle Eastern descent standing next to a small airplane that displayed US registry. The US Department of Homeland Security maintained continuous surveillance of the plane that had been located at the Knoxville airport within two hours of Frank's observation. USDHS was not aware that before they initiated their own surveillance, Frank had located the airplane, installed a solar-activated global positioning system, and packed enough explosives to ensure the aircraft would only reach a destination that was acceptable to the US government. The plane was registered in the name of American States Bloc. Intelligence analysts had quickly decided that the first letters of the registry (ASB) probably should be interpreted as Ali Salim Bakara. One linguist on the NSA analytical team had immediately pointed out that "bloc" is a coalition of people, groups, or nations with the same purpose or goal. Could Ali Salim Bloc be the name of a new organization that at some point planned to leave a footprint or crater on American soil?

Simultaneous to the efforts being conducted by NSA, the FBI had determined that the red, white, and blue painted Cessna 172 in question had last filed a flight plan six weeks previously for a flight to the Fulton County Airport in Atlanta. Records of the Federal Aviation Administration (FAA) had indicated the flight plan was submitted by one Ashram Bakara, who had stated that his purpose of the trip was to practice touch-and-go flying procedures.

Ongoing investigation had revealed that Ashram Bakara had graduated from Gatlinburg-Pittman High School in Gatlinburg, Tennessee, three years previously. His school records reflected that his parents were Ali S. and Fatima Bakara.

The FBI actively searched for the current location of Ashram to ensure he too could be placed under the umbrella of surveillance.

Chapter 60

Kirk was not surprised when he learned from Lennie Oathmeyer that Nur Jasmin had been placed on a deep cover assignment and wouldn't be reporting to the office for several months. There were plenty of desks inside the office, and yet Kirk had only met Frank and Nur. The only reassuring sign to Kirk was the fact that Lois had not emptied the contents of Nur's desk.

Lennie did not mention the ongoing investigation in Pigeon Forge with the exception of telling Kirk that he had done an excellent job in establishing the cover story that had been adjusted for Frank Gayle, who was, as Oathmeyer described it, "still pounding a beat on ole rocky top."

Kirk took the opportunity of not being on an active assignment to develop cover documents for future roles that would require identity changes. While conducting his preparatory work, it dawned on the young agent that he had more identities than many police informants who were living under a blanket of obscurity in the federal witness protection program. Within a short time, Alexander possessed driver's licenses, voter registration cards, and numerous credit cards that had been issued to several assorted names across the United States.

"With enough time," thought Kirk, "I could control an entire election and get a good Republican administration back in office." Kirk was rapidly becoming a master in stealing or creating identities.

Chapter 61

The mystery surrounding the location of Ashram Bakara was short lived in the intelligence community. An early morning phone call from a prepaid cellular phone that originated in Frankfort, Germany, was monitored by agents from both the CIA and the FBI. Ali Salim Bakara learned that his son, Ashram, had been successful in his "business" matters and would be arriving in two days.

Within thirty minutes, the Department of Homeland Security was able to confirm that one Ashram Bakara, a naturalized US citizen, had secured a business-class reservation on Flight 1176 that would leave Frankfort the following morning for Chicago, where Bakara was scheduled for a connecting flight that would fly him to the airport in Knoxville, Tennessee.

Simultaneous to the efforts of Homeland Security, intelligence analysts from the NSA secured credit card receipts in the name of Ashram Bakara in an effort to establish a paper trail of the places he had visited during his travel outside the United States.

One clue that surfaced almost immediately was the fact that Ashram had spent two days at the Ramada Plaza Hotel in Karachi, Pakistan. Hotel records indicated that he had checked out of his room at 10:17 a.m. the previous Wednesday, and airline records he had boarded a flight to Frankfort at 5:50 p.m. Perhaps it was too coincidental that at 12:44 p.m., a car that contained explosives had been detonated outside the U S consulate in Karachi.

Within a two-hour period, Ashram Bakara had raised from obscurity, bypassed being a person of interest, and had been classified by the US government as a suspected terrorist.

Chapter 62

The phone call from Ashram to his father had triggered a flurry of activity, both from within the Mountain Rapids Motel and at global intelligence agencies throughout Europe and the Middle East.

Surveillance video from inside and around the Ramada Plaza Hotel was in the hands of CIA agents who were inside a small office at the American consulate in Karachi comparing hotel video to embassy video recordings of the car that had exploded near American soil. Analysts had already determined that Ashram Bakara had observed the explosion from a block away. Video that had been taken from myriad cameras within the American consulate and Ramada Plaza Hotel confirmed that the car that had exploded was driven by a Middle Eastern male who had met Ashram at the hotel. The then unknown male had then driven to the parking area near the consulate, where it was abandoned and had exploded twelve minutes later.

While agents in Karachi were performing their due diligence, investigators from the FBI had located Ashram Bakara's car parked in the extended parking area at the Knoxville airport and had installed tracking devices and transmitters that would ensure government operatives would not have to exert more work other than pressing a few buttons to know exactly where Ashrams car was located.

Chapter 63

Lennie Oathmeyer had just concluded a series of conference calls with his counterparts from within the intelligence community and was in the process of briefing Senator Wingate.

"Son," said the senator, "hang by your phone. I need to have a heart to heart with POTUS."

Within fifteen minutes Wingate returned the call. "The president of the United States and I are in full concurrence on a solution to this mountain thing," Wingate stated. "The last thing we need is a terrorist act, or even a threat of terrorism, surfacing in that area. Once we know with certainty that something bad is being planned, you're directed to have your boys eliminate the threat. Its damned time that some of these Arabs start shedding some tears that are painted red, white, and blue."

"There's nothing like senatorial revenge," thought Oathmeyer as he hung up the phone and instructed Lois to locate Kirk Alexander and have him report to the office immediately.

Chapter 64

Ashram Bakara no longer just hated Americans; he now also considered anyone from Germany as his lifelong enemy. This new attitude was based on the treatment he'd received while proceeding through the screening process to board his Lufthansa flight to Chicago. Bakara had been screened, directed to a secondary screening area for a more in-depth examination, and then questioned about his travel activities prior to finally being allowed to board his flight. His carefully packed carry-on luggage was in shambles, and Ashram realized that there was no item in his suitcase that had escaped close scrutiny of Frankfort Airport security.

Ashram would have become extremely paranoid if he had known that the passenger in the adjacent seat and the one immediately behind his assigned seat were in fact heavily armed agents whose only purpose in life was to surround potential threats on airlines to ensure the flight remained uneventful. Their instructions were clear: "If he as much as burps aboard the flight, break his neck immediately."

The Lufthansa flight was smooth, and the flight attendant was considerate enough to request travelers with connecting flights exit the plane first. As was normal in the airline industry, this was a request that was completely ignored. However, Ashram was able to reach his next flight with thirty minutes to spare.

Another passenger, an elderly gentleman with thick glasses, white hair, and enough crevices along his aged face to resemble the Grand Canyon, also boarded the flight to Knoxville. Just hours before, this passenger had arrived from Dulles Airport, following a detailed briefing that had originated in the Oval Office of 1600 Pennsylvania Avenue in Washington DC.

Kirk Alexander was ready to get down and dirty with the enemy.

Chapter 65

While Ashram Bakara was retrieving his own luggage before walking to his vehicle at the Knoxville airport, Kirk had walked directly to the front door at the departing passenger's gate, where he was met by an agent from the FBI. The agent handed Kirk the keys to a late model pickup truck that was parked at the curb. It only took a matter of minutes for Kirk to be briefed on the various instruments that were installed in the grey Chevrolet truck. A GPS displayed a red arrow and a green one. The red was the 2007 black Buick owned by Ashram. The green arrow displayed Kirk's location in proximity to the terrorist's vehicle. While getting his own briefing, Kirk heard the sound of a vehicle being started on a speaker that was mounted above the driver's seat.

"That's our target," advised the FBI operative. "Any sound coming from within the target vehicle is being monitored and recorded by our personnel. Hopefully you understand Arabic."

Fortunately, Kirk had received specialized training on the equipment that his own vehicle contained and didn't need additional instructions. He put his vehicle in gear at the exact moment that Bakara's vehicle began to move and thanked his counterpart for his assistance.

Before Kirk left the confines of the airport, he had removed his glasses and wig, and displayed a completely new identify that Bakara would not recognize in the event he'd noticed Alexander at any point during the flight. Kirk was well versed in this type of activity and was close to certain that at no time had Ashram given him more than a second glance.

If Ashram Bakara's first mistake was being on a terrorist watch list, his second was the cellular phone call he made to his father while leaving the airport—and one which Kirk listened to and completely understood.

"Happy seventy-fifth," said Ashram to his father, who had been expecting a call from his son. "I'm on the way and should be home within an hour."

"We have important guests coming tonight," replied Bakara to his son. The phone conversation was ended without a good-bye or additional talk.

There are times in life when the least said can carry the most important messages. This proved to be one of those times. Within minutes there was a flurry of phone activity between NSA, FBI, Homeland Security, and CIA. When briefed by Lennie Oathmeyer, Senator Royal T. Wingate wasted no time in notifying the president of the information that had just been intercepted. The reality of the unfolding events was rapidly being assessed by numerous operatives within the intelligence network of the country.

In two days, on September 2, the Great Smoky Mountain National Park (GSMNP) would be celebrating the seventy-fifth anniversary of the park, which had been originally dedicated by former President Franklin D. Roosevelt. Even the president of the United States was contemplating attending the event, where guests including the governors of both Tennessee and North Carolina, the secretary of the interior, senators and congressional elected officials, and high school bands from both states would be in attendance. The event would also be honoring descendants of many of the original pioneers who had settled in the Smoky Mountain region. In short, as one government analyst claimed, this event would be a prime target that would bring tourism to a virtual standstill for the region, as well as almost all of the national parks throughout the country.

Inside his own office, Senator Royal T. Wingate read the words of former Secretary of the Interior, Harold L. Ickes, who had been one of the guest speakers on September 2, 1940, at the Newfound Gap dedication of the park.

"National Parks are authentic, democratic American products. God gave us rare treasures of natural beauty, and we Americans are doing our humble best to be worthy of the gift by preserving and cherishing all that we can of it for the enjoyment and inspiration of all the people," Ickes had stated.

"Mr. Secretary," the senator softly said. "I assure you that what God gave us will live longer than those who want to take the gift from us."

Chapter 66

When Kirk had done his original planning for his anticipated trip to Pigeon Forge, Tennessee, he had utilized the virtual reality program in learning the layout of the area. He realized as he followed Ashram Bakara along the winding roads leading toward the Smoky Mountains that he was still familiar with the area.

Kirk noted the red arrow on his GPS had pulled into a parking lot and stopped. Ashram had just arrived at his father's motel.

Kirk parked his own vehicle a block from the motel at a fast food joint and took the opportunity to contact Lennie in Washington.

"Kirk, I want you to stay close to the target and keep me informed of anything that happens," Lennie directed. "We have a meeting that will start here at 5:30 p.m., and we will be monitoring a live feed from our assets that are concealed at the target area. We're hoping that tonight's activities will disclose some telling information about your assignment, and there's reason to believe you may need to get your hands dirty."

Lennie maintained a policy of only sharing the information one of his operatives may need to perform his duties. He had been advised by Frank Gale earlier in the day that Ali Salim Bakara had given him a day off, with pay. Frank had also been instructed by Oathmeyer to remain available in the event his talents were needed.

Additionally, at 5:30 p.m., Lennie would meet with Frank Sanders of the FBI, Matthew Hellerman of CIA, and Admiral Delia of NSA, where they would sit in on the important meeting that Ali Bakara had mentioned to his son.

Leonard Oathmeyer reviewed a list he had prepared in anticipation of the pending meeting.

1. Ali Salim Bakara had maintained contact with known terrorists in Paris.
2. Ashram Bakara had been in contact with a terrorist in Karachi immediately prior to a bombing outside the US consulate, and he had witnessed the explosion.
3. Both of the Bakaras were known to use cellular phones with prepaid calling, a popular practice among terrorist organizations.
4. Ashram had stated "Happy seventy-fifth," believed to be a reference to a planned attack.
5. Ashram was a licensed pilot and had immediate access to a plane.
6. When Ashram's baggage was inspected in Frankfort, a copy of the *Tennessee Star Journal* was inside the computer case. This particular issue provided extensive news coverage and the itinerary of the seventy-fifth anniversary of the GSMNP, which would be celebrated on September 2.
7. Reminder: September 11 was another significant day for the United States.

One additional piece of information that Oathmeyer possessed was the fact that when his own operative, Frank, had been hired at the Mountain Rapids Motel, Ali Bakara had stated that room 111 was a VIP suite. During the preceding two days, Ali had been observed on the clandestine monitoring equipment as he placed soft drinks in the refrigerator of the room, an indication that he was preparing for a VIP visit.

Chapter 67

At 5:20 p.m. Lennie Oathmeyer entered the office of Admiral Thurmont Delia, where his counterparts from the intelligence community were already seated. A large television was at one end of a large desk and color showed in brilliant the interior of room 111 at the Mountain Rapids Motel. A second television displayed a series of real-time camera shots of the motel office, parking area, pool area, and several rooms that appeared to be vacant.

"Your team did an excellent job on installing the cameras, Lennie," stated Director Sanders of the FBI.

"Thanks, Frank, I'll pass that on to them," Lennie responded.

The group sat around the table, waiting to determine if a meeting was going to actually take place at the motel and exchanging individual views on the ongoing investigation. The entire group agreed with Lennie's assessment on the probability of the Bakara family being actively engaged in a terrorist enterprise.

At 6:25 p.m. a Dodge Durango SUV pulled into the parking lot of the motel, and two men who appeared to be of Middle Eastern descent got out of the vehicle and were met and hugged by Ali Bakara and his son before they hurried from the office.

"Time to get the interpreter," stated Admiral Delia as he pushed a button on his desk. A young lady immediately entered the room, put on a set of ear phones, and sat next to the television. The admiral then handed a set of ear phones to each of the gathered department heads. "Gentlemen, my assistant, Carolyn, will interpret the conversation if it's in Arabic, and the only voice we will hear will be hers as she translates. I have two other interpreters in the adjacent office who will record and transcribe the contents of the conversations."

As the gathering of intelligence officers watched, the suspected terrorists walked out of camera view, and seconds later they were observed on the widescreen television as they entered room 111.

"Allah is blessed," stated Carolyn as the terrorist group sat down around a table and began conversing in Arabic. It was apparent that the meeting belonged to Ali Salim Bakara.

"A few days ago, my son, Ashram, struck a blow to the infidels in Pakistan. Today, praise Allah, I am giving you both the opportunity to sit beside Allah as martyrs, served by those long-awaited virgins who will instill happiness in your hearts while serving your needs," Bakara stated.

Smiles broke out on the faces of the intelligence officials as they realized, as one, that they were listening to the actual planning of an act of terrorism that they would be able to prevent.

"In two days there will be a celebration just a few miles from here that the infidels will use to honor their theft of property from their own people. It will be attended by officials from the infidel government and hundreds of tourists who will bring their cameras. Ahmet and Nayan, you will give them something big and beautiful to photograph. You both will be martyrs that the world remembers and thanks."

As the plans unfolded, Lennie wrote copious notes that he knew he needed to share with Senator Wingate before the night was over. He just hoped that the meeting at the motel would carry on past the time for the senator's beloved Jeopardy.

Ahmet was a bus driver who worked for a company providing charter services throughout the mountain region. He had been designated to drive newspaper reporters and media personnel from Patriot Park in Pigeon Forge to the dedication site near Clingman's Dome. Prior to meeting his passengers, Ahmet would drive to the motel, where Ali Salim Bakara would be waiting with Nayan and Ashram. They would remove four hundred pounds of explosives from the basement area of the motel and place it in the luggage area of the bus. Both Nayan and Ahmet would ride in the bus transporting passengers, with Ahmet as the driver and Nayan as a news representative. Bakara also advised that both Nayan and Ahmet would possess detonators that would be activated during the playing of the national anthem.

Lennie Oathmeyer had heard enough of the planning to realize the group needed to make immediate notifications to the highest echelons of the US government, and the other agency directors shared that sentiment. Lennie made a conference call to Senator Wingate as the perplexed intelligence overseers listened. Unknown to the agency leaders was the fact that the president of the United States would be monitoring the briefing.

"Lennie," asked the senator after hearing the plans of the terrorist group, "Is there any doubt in your mind that their plan could work?"

"Sir, we are all in complete concurrence that tonight is our premier opportunity to eliminate this particular threat, either through a tactical response that would create panic throughout the United States, or through a catastrophic accident that could be carried out by our dirty boys, with no national scare and short-lived publicity."

There was a pause as the gathered intelligence officers listened to Senator Wingate in conversation with someone else. After two minutes he returned to his conference call. "Lennie, inform NSA, CIA, and FBI to stand down immediately and have their personnel vacate the area," the senator stated. "The president has elected to allow the dirty boys do what they know best."

Directors Hellerman of the CIA, Director Sanders of the FBI, and Admiral Delia of the NSA nodded their heads when the directive was given.

"You've got the bull by the horns, Lennie," stated the Admiral. "God bless, and good luck." Again the men nodded in agreement.

Within minutes individual agency heads were notifying their ground personnel to terminate their activities immediately, pack up their equipment, and return to their regularly assigned duty posts for further instructions. The only exception to this flurry of activity was on the part of Leonard Oathmeyer, who had notified Kirk and Frank to meet at Frank's room at the Cold Creek Resort and wait for a conference call from himself.

An intelligence analyst was brought in to monitor the activities at the motel on the video monitors to ensure none of the principal players left the motel.

Chapter 68

Frank Gale, who had been living under the assumed name of Alex Strait, was glad to see Kirk. The two would have enjoyed going out to have a few beers together, but when one was waiting for a directive from your superior, there was no such thing as a timeout for cocktail hour.

Their cellular phone rang at the same time. It would obviously be Leonard Oathmeyer with important instructions. "Frank, how soon can you create a major explosion at the motel?" asked Lennie.

"I can make a catastrophe happen within ten minutes, boss," Gale replied. "I have enough explosives tied in to a natural gas line that the whole building would be decimated within three seconds."

It was also determined that only one room in the motel was rented to a man and his wife who were visiting Pigeon Forge. Lennie had already confirmed that FBI surveillance had followed the couple from the motel to the Dixie Stampede Dinner Show. That show would not end for another forty-five minutes.

"I want you and Kirk to level that damned motel with the current occupants—who, by the way, are confirmed terrorists that have targeted the dedication of the national park when the events are held tomorrow," Lennie directed.

"We'll be there within five minutes," Frank stated.

"Set it off in ten minutes," Lennie replied. "I have one notification to make."

Exactly nine minutes later, Frank entered the maintenance area of the Mountain Rapids Motel. He walked to a corner and moved a trash can that concealed a small timer affixed to a C-5 explosive packet. The entire packet was affixed to a natural gas pipe a mere six inches away. Frank set the timer for four minutes and walked casually back to the pickup truck where Kirk was waiting to drive the two from the motel.

They pulled up to the drive-through window of a fast food place a block away when the entire area was rocked by an explosion of unbelievable force, immediately followed by a secondary explosion that spread splinter-sized pieces of the motel and miniscule fragments of body parts throughout the area.

In the aftermath of the explosion which was believed by the news to have killed an entire family of hard-working, naturalized citizens from Afghanistan, Code Enforcement Officer Roger Fleming of Sevier County, Tennessee, perhaps summed up the incident best and removed any doubts of suspicious activity involved in the horrific accident. Fleming was on the scene of the incident within minutes of the explosion and informed gathering news reporters that he had recently cited the owner for numerous unsafe practices that could lead to an explosion. "I suggested to Mr. Bakara that he hire a professional to maintain the safety of his motel," Fleming was quoted by a local reporter. "He was apparently more concerned with saving money than investing in the services of some company that would keep his property safe for his family and the millions of tourist who visit this great place."

The day following the explosion, over a thousand guests, VIPs, and reporters gathered at the jubilant seventy-fifth anniversary celebration of GSMNP, where famed Sevier County singer Dolly Parton entertained the gathering.

While Dolly was entertaining her fans, the Department of Homeland Security was quietly seizing a small airplane from the airport in Knoxville, courtesy of a small terrorist organization that never had the opportunity to inflict damage or eat mom's apple pie.

Chapter 69

Lennie Oathmeyer had long known that when the president of the United States was happy and Senator Royal T. Wingate was happy, then *he* was ecstatic.

The president had carefully monitored any reports that related to the motel explosion of unknown origin. It was obvious that the entire matter had been reported just as one of those horrible events that can and did occur.

Lennie was especially pleased with how his old friend Roger Fleming had stepped to the plate and explained the explosion to reporters in such a way that press accounts indicated that the chain of tragic events rested directly on the shoulders of Ali Salim Bakara.

Senator Royal Wingate was not one who overlooked any opportunity to increase his power and sphere of influence. He had already decided that if an attack at a national park had been contemplated once, it would surface again. In the mind of Wingate, the POTUS should have someone at the helm of the Department of Interior who was tough-minded, proficient, and willing to go that extra mile in service of their country. He shared his feelings with Leonard Oathmeyer, who immediately responded with what Wingate recognized as a way of promoting his own trusted people to powerful positions.

"Senator, my suggestion would be to have Polly Gregory appointed as Secretary of the Interior, and hire Leslie McCarter, The Broom, to take over the Bureau of Prisons, which would truly mean that leadership of BOP is completely aware of the full scope of their responsibilities," Lennie stated. "With me continuing as your assistant and running the activities of the dirty squad, you have picked up two layers of added responsibility."

Leonard Oathmeyer was well aware that his boss would interpret the layers of responsibility as layers of power, words by which the senator lived.

"I'm going to give that suggestion some careful thought, son," the senator said. Wingate knew that the current secretary of the interior, Stan Blemish, was a hold over from the previous administration and had been retained by the president only as a personal favor to Senator David Leatherwood, who had died of a heart attack a few months previously.

Polly Gregory could talk for hours about her pride and love for her two sons while having the ability to share minutes when she would discuss twenty-seven miserable years of marriage. The native of St. Louis had shared her wit and wisdom with friends while living in St. Louis; Gatlinburg, Tennessee; Alpharetta, Georgia; and finally Washington DC, where she had found her niche in the Bureau of Prisons, starting in a lower level and worked her way to the position of director.

Senator Royal T. Wingate took pride in rewarding those who had supported him in his political career, and Polly led the list, although on several occasions she had caused him to take deep breaths of air—and on one occasion, a near stroke. That occasion had been when Gregory was preparing to testify to Congress on her budget request for the BOP, an openly gay senator, known to have disdain and reservations about women in higher positions in government, expressed a comment that he didn't feel a woman was capable of overseeing prisons that were overflowing with violent men.

Polly Gregory had smiled at the senator and stated, "Senator, those men in prison think with their penis, and I believe that some of our elected congressmen and senators see through their penis. Now, I hope you're not going to be known as 'short sighted.'"

The senator had elected not to challenge any item in the projected budget, yet Senator Wingate could see that he might surface as a devil in the details on her appointment as secretary of the interior. But as usual, Wingate had a plan.

Before Wingate would approach the president on the merits of a cabinet change, he needed to ensure that his counterpart in Congress was on board for her confirmation. His answer was only a phone call away.

"Larry," Senator Wingate said to the liberal congressman from New York, "I just wanted to give you a heads-up on Polly Gregory, the lady that the president is thinking of appointing to take over as secretary of the interior.

Congressman Larry Barker, the gay representative from New York, immediately cringed when he heard the name Polly Gregory. "I wasn't aware the president was anticipating a change," Barker stated.

"It's a closely held card that only a few of us are aware of," Wingate replied. He continued to explain that an inmate being held in the federal detention center in Charleston, South Carolina, had been telling lies regarding a sexual relationship he claimed to have had with Congressman Barker.

"Polly Gregory told me that she wasn't about to have the name of an honorable person such as you impugned," Wingate lied. "She shipped his ass to Big Max, in Denver."

Congressman Larry Barker was well aware that Big Max was the most dreaded facility in the entire country. He also knew that there could in fact be reality in the statements that Royal Wingate was making. "I sure don't need those kinds of lies going around," Barker noted. "And for the record, I strongly support the appointment of Gregory."

The senator hung up the phone and decided it was time to put a bug in the ear of the POTUS, whose first question was, "Royal, isn't Gregory the one who kicked the *USA Today* reporter in the, uh, testicles?"

"No, sir," responded Wingate. "She only threatened to kick him."

Before the conversation ended, the president agreed on the merits of the appointment and assured the senator that his staff would arrange for the resignation of the current secretary of the interior.

"Who was instrumental in getting the secretary of interior appointed, Alex?" thought the senator as he remembered that he needed to be home to watch his favorite show that evening.

Chapter 70

Kirk and Frank had decided to return to Washington together after confirming with Lennie that they could return the truck Kirk had used to the Washington Field Office of the FBI. The trip gave the two covert agents an opportunity to become better acquainted.

They were in high spirits as they traveled on Interstate 81 toward the city of Washington. Before leaving Pigeon Forge, Frank had been thoroughly debriefed by agents from the FBI. Both he and Kirk knew they would be returning to work where again they would be thoroughly interviewed and analyzed by CIA psychiatrists before receiving orders for their next assignment.

"The interviews should be simple for me," Kirk stated. "All I did was drive the get-away vehicle."

"Just hope they don't retire you because of road rage," Frank joked. "I won't get away so easy. I just killed the entire terrorist nation that was living in Tennessee."

As the two sped through the horse country surrounding Charlottesville, Virginia, they never imagined that at that moment Lennie Oathmeyer was reviewing an intelligence report that could put at least one of their lives in serious danger.

Chapter 71

Polly Gregory was sitting at her desk in complete and utter shock. She had just been informed by the president's chief of staff that the president wanted to appoint her to a cabinet position leading the department of interior as their fiftieth appointed secretary.

Gregory realized that this appointment, if confirmed by the US Senate, would place her in the eighth position to succeed the POTUS in the event of his death. She also recognized the fact that most appointments to this respected position of government were natives of Western states. Polly's secret weapon was the fact that for several years she'd owned a fifteen-acre piece of land that was just a few miles from Taos, New Mexico.

Although the chief of staff emphasized that his role was to advise her of the president's desires, it would be the president himself who would make the offer.

Polly had responded that she would be honored to be recommended and thrilled if confirmed, and she would do her utmost to ensure any critics would know that the president had made a wise choice in his selection.

With this knowledge in hand, the chief of staff had contacted the current secretary of interior, Stan Blemish, and suggested that he consider retirement because he didn't fit into some of the plans the president had for the post.

Blemish was a master at the intricate game of politics and realized the POTUS had been more than kind in keeping him on in his position, despite a change of leadership at the helm of government. Within an hour, Blemish had proffered his resignation to the president and in a traditional political response had learned that his resignation had been "reluctantly" accepted by the commander in chief.

Polly's anticipated phone call from the president came early in the afternoon; she was requested to be at the White House in an hour to discuss plans relating to an anticipated change in the cabinet.

By 5:30 p.m., Polly Gregory had met with the POTUS for the first time and informed him she would gladly serve his office in any way or position that she could.

"In order to assure the Congress that I've put careful thought into your appointment, I'm going to wait a few days to submit your name," the president stated.

The two agreed that Polly would not submit her resignation as director of the Bureau of Prisons until she was confirmed by the US Senate for the post.

Chapter 72

Lennie Oathmeyer and Greg Wilson sat inside Lennie's Capitol Hill office. Lennie was in possession of a top secret intelligence report that had been received at CIA Headquarters, and he wanted straight advice on how to proceed. Oathmeyer knew there was no one in the US government who would be more candid than Wilson.

"A few weeks ago our American consulate in Karachi experienced a car bombing on the street outside the embassy," Lennie said. "One of the suspects was linked to a Taliban organization that was being operated here in the United States. The individual from America met with an unfortunate accident after returning to this country. The interesting aspect is that the other individual from Karachi—the one who parked the vehicle borne incendiary explosive device, incidentally—apparently heard that the other suspect had been killed during an explosion in Tennessee. For some reason, the suspect who had planted the vehicle got the idea that our government was behind the accident. This Memen Al-Jibouri decided he was next in line for an unfortunate accident, and so he contacted the consulate in Karachi and began talking."

Oathmeyer then handed Wilson a seven-page statement that had been provided by Memen to CIA personnel who were assigned to monitor activities in Pakistan.

Greg Wilson read the contents of the statement and smiled broadly. "Lennie, what you have is a terrorist organization that's running scared," Wilson stated. "He mentions the two incidents in Paris and the one in Tennessee as his proof that the US government has declared their own aggressive war on combating terrorism, and yet the Taliban has no proof, just suspicion. In short, our tactics are beginning to work against the enemy."

The contents of the statement that had been given by Memen reflected that because an entire family of terrorists had died in Tennessee, he was personally afraid that his own family could be mysteriously killed in an accident. The two agents realized that Memen Al-Jibouri was negotiating for the preservation of his own family, even if it meant sacrificing his other family, his terrorist family.

Although Memen Al-Jibouri had managed to fly under the radar screen of known intelligence operations, his statement showed enough knowledge of terrorist activities to make him worthwhile to the US government. Leonard Oathmeyer recommended to the CIA that rather than targeting Al-Jibouri, he should be recruited for an undercover informant role and be allowed to live as long as his information breathed life into the ongoing counterterrorist program.

Chapter 73

Kirk Alexander and Frank Gale immediately recognized that something serious was amiss in the office after they returned from Tennessee. Lennie Oathmeyer, although extremely complimentary and praising on the outcome in Pigeon Forge, seemed distracted by other issues that weren't immediately apparent to his staff. Even Lois Harding seemed troubled, which was a totally new image that no one in the office had previously observed.

"When he figures out his solutions, he'll be sharing it all with us," Gale stated. "That's just the nature of Lennie's personality."

While Oathmeyer was sorting out the demons in his own mind, Kirk and Frank went through the routine procedure of debriefing, mental and physical examinations, and the endless task of report submissions. One enterprising government psychologist, following his extensive interview process, closed his report with a complete deviation from medical jargon. "They're just as fit as a couple of Tennessee fiddles," he stated in his final evaluation.

Following the completion of the fitness procedures, Lennie called Kirk and Frank into his office. "You guys have been working extremely hard and under some of the most trying situations you could be exposed to," he stated. "I want you both to take a couple of weeks off to enjoy life."

Frank Gale wasted no time in bidding good-bye and heading toward the door of the office. Kirk, on the other hand, returned to his desk and sat contemplatively. Although Kirk was aware that he had no immediate assignments, he took the advantage of free time to work on new identities that he would surely need in the future.

After working for a period of time, Kirk left the office, returned to his apartment, and packed enough clothing for a few days of travel. An hour later he was at the Union Train Station in Washington, waiting to board an Amtrak train to New York City.

Chapter 74

Nur Jasmin was fully recovered from the facial reconstruction she'd received through the skilled hands of a Rhode Island surgeon. She still possessed the exotic beauty that was frequently found on the faces of women of Middle Eastern descent, but at the suggestion of her physician, she had her hair lightened, which would allow her to pose as a valley girl from the beaches of sunny California. Weeks of intense physical exercise at the private sanitarium had also ensured that Nur could easily star in the swimsuit edition of *Sports Illustrated*.

At the very moment that Leonard Oathmeyer was instructing his intelligence operatives to take some time off, Nur was being instructed by her doctor that she was being officially discharged to return to her assigned duties with the government.

She called Lennie Oathmeyer to share the news of her discharge.

"Take the next week off and report back for duty a week from Monday," Lennie instructed.

Nur realized that she had several days to enjoy life before reporting back to work. She walked outside of the hospital into the garden, took a small cellular phone from her slacks pocket, and made a short phone call.

Following the completion of her call, Nur smiled and walked back to her room, where she hastily packed for her departure from Rhode Island. "A new face and a new life," she thought as she placed her clothes into a small suitcase.

Chapter 75

Kirk had enjoyed the train ride from Washington to New York. As the train passed Lanham, a short distance from his childhood home of Bowie, Kirk thought back to his happy and youthful days. He would accompany his father, who played softball with the Fraternal Order of Police and would spend his days off in practice, while his son, Kirk Jr., proudly watched from the sidelines.

As the Amtrak pulled into Penn Station in downtown Manhattan, it dawned on Kirk that he'd never had the opportunity to visit what was purportedly the most exciting city in the world. He had to fight the surge of excitement as he walked up the steps from the station to appreciate what many of his recent past targets had given their own lives to destroy.

While on the train heading toward New York, Kirk had called the Hilton Times Square Hotel and made reservations for a corner room with a king-sized bed. While confirming his reservations, he also learned that the concierge would be able to obtain last-minute tickets for almost any Broadway performance that Kirk may wish to attend.

When he walked up the steps from the arrival platform to street level, Kirk realized that New York was a city where a tourist should faithfully practice personal security procedures. The derelicts and addicts encountered throughout the terminal were grim reminders that criminals who sought opportunity would find the horn of plenty immediately below Madison Square Garden.

Kirk Alexander realized as he walked that he was using training from an almost forgotten training school that had instructed the students on the ability to display an air of ability and confidence as opposed to an air of insecurity. No one had approached Kirk as the final rays of sunlight met his eyes.

The ride to the hotel was quick despite the heavy traffic in midtown Manhattan, and with the exception of receiving one phone call while driving down West Forty-second Street toward his hotel, Kirk had the opportunity to appreciate the hustle and bustle of Times Square.

Following hotel registration and while riding the elevator to the seventh floor, it dawned on Kirk that it had been many years since he'd registered at a hotel under his own identity. Security planning had again played a role in registration; he had requested any floor from floor nine and below to ensure he would be in a location that could be accessed by a fire department ladder truck in the event of unforeseen emergencies.

Chapter 76

Kirk had showered after unpacking his small suitcase and was sitting on a couch watching Fox News when he heard a small knock at his door. He immediately walked to the peep hole and looked out before opening the door.

"As Salaam Alaykum," Nur Jasim stated while smiling broadly.

"Wa Alaykum As-Salamm," he replied as she entered the door and melted into his arms. For the next several hours, their communications progressed from the language of Arabic to the language of love. Eventually, their spent bodies confirmed the two lovers were proficient in both languages.

Throughout Nur's hospitalization and recovery, Kirk had found the opportunities to visit her on several occasions. Despite the Bureau of Prison's strict doctrine on interoffice relationships, Kirk had found the time and suitable disguises, which enabled him to visit Nur for short periods of time, personally check on her well-being and recovery, and then proceed to whatever assignment Lennie Oathmeyer had delegated.

"What do you think Lennie would say if he knew about us?" Nur asked.

Kirk thought for a full minute before responding. "I believe he would instruct The Broom to create two vacancies within the Bureau of Prisons." Unknown to Lennie Oathmeyer was the fact that Kirk had determined the location of Nur from a memo Lennie had forgotten was to file.

Ironically, a late-night repeat of an earlier press conference caught the attention of both Nur and Kirk when they heard the report that Polly Ann Gregory of the BOP had been nominated by the president as secretary of the interior. The news release went on to report that Congressman

Larry Barker, the flamboyant congressional leader from New York, had immediately gone on record by stating, "This is an excellent selection at a time when hundreds of thousands of gallons of crude oil are flooding the clean waters of the Gulf of Mexico. Ms. Gregory needs to be confirmed quickly so she can start kicking some butt in our troubled waters."

"For some reason, I just don't think either of us will be named to replace Polly Gregory," Nur stated. "I've seen her in action, and she's the equivalent to being a bulldog at a hot dog fight."

Sleep came easily as they relaxed in each other's arms.

Chapter 77

Throughout the weekend, Senator Royal T. Wingate lobbied his colleagues on behalf of a rapid confirmation for Polly Gregory's appointment. It was soon apparent that opposition would be minimal, and Lennie Oathmeyer was instructed to ensure a suitable replacement for Gregory was in place and ready to assume duties as director of the Bureau of Prisons. This task was becoming somewhat of an enigma to Oathmeyer. Leslie McCarter relished his position as an occasional soldier of fortune and was reluctant to return to a life of order, sensibility, and civility.

"Lennie, you just can't take an old broom and turn it into a bulldozer," McCarter stated. "The Bureau of Prisons needs a bulldozer, not an old, worn-out bull crapper."

Oathmeyer never found much humor in being refused when his own mind was made up, yet he intellectually realized that The Broom was an old soldier who would fight to retain a set of fatigues rather than wear a three-piece suit. He understood the mandate of having a BOP director who realized the importance of that position and had the wherewithal to deal with the almost insurmountable issues that were created on a daily basis. The penal institutions throughout the country were becoming breeding grounds for homegrown terrorists, lacking in rehabilitative programs and releasing criminals back into society at a higher proficiency level to generate more crime. Oathmeyer almost wished he hadn't recommended Polly Gregory for a cabinet position; her loss created a void that he had to fill.

When the name Greg Wilson popped up in his mind, Oathmeyer smiled broadly. Wilson was perhaps a better choice for Bureau of Prisons than anyone he could imagine, including McCarter. Although direct in his personal dealings, Wilson could be diplomatic, decisive, and convincing. He had a total grasp of tasks he was involved in, was excellent at multitasking, and would not hesitate to make life miserable for anyone who had harmed, or was capable of harming, the interests of the United States.

A quick phone call from Oathmeyer was all that was needed to arrange a 3:00 p.m. meeting at Lennie's Capitol Hill office.

Greg Wilson was aware of the pending vacancy and realized that if he were to be offered the post, his friend Polly Gregory would do everything possible to ensure his transition would be easy.

Four hours later, Wilson had accepted an offer to direct the Bureau of Prisons and went home for a satisfying drink, while Lennie Oathmeyer went to a cocktail party on Capitol Hill, pleased with the knowledge that he'd drained another cesspool in the swamp of democracy.

Chapter 78

For four days, Nur and Kirk enjoyed New York City as only two lovers could appreciate. They faithfully followed an agenda of Broadway shows, Radio City Music Hall, endless sex, and never-ending conversation .

They were passengers on a harbor cruise boat when Nur stated, "I'd like to leave this sordid life before someone takes our lives."

"The problem is, if we choose to leave this life, Lennie would have no choice but to direct someone to take us out," Kirk candidly replied.

The two stood in awkward silence, observing the Statute of Liberty while contemplating the predicament that would face them if a wrong decision was made.

"Perhaps I could just ask Lennie for a compassionate transfer to some other agency," she suggested. "I could tell him, and with truthfulness, that my kidnapping has left me unsure of myself. Kirk, I want to spend my life with you creating life—not destroying it."

Kirk held her tightly, realizing that no response was expected. Finally he answered, "I'm in love with you, Nur."

"As I am with you, my prince," she replied.

The two would not discuss their situation further because they had one night left in the city that never slept, and the two wanted to ensure they lived up to the words of that song.

The following morning they took separate trains back to Washington for security purposes. Nur ensured she took a train whose travels had originated in Rhode Island.

Although Nur was scheduled to report to work the following Monday morning, Kirk had another week off, and he decided he'd rather spend it in the DC area, close to the one with whom he had fallen in love.

Chapter 79

As scheduled, Nur Jasmin returned to her office at the BOP the following Monday. She spent most of the morning reviewing intelligence reports that had arrived from various intelligence groups within the government.

Lennie Oathmeyer, although seeing some similarity in the new face, was confident that Nur could continue her intelligence activities without being recognized.

He did come into her office during the late morning hours to advise her that for the following two days, she should report directly to the CIA facility in Langley for refresher course with firearms and self-defense techniques. This was routine procedure for an agent who had been away from their assignments for a period of time.

Nur was only too happy to engage in activities away from the office because it suddenly felt somewhat strange to be in the environment where so much death and destruction was planned.

Prior to leaving New York, Kirk and Nur had purchased cellular phones with prepaid calling accessibility because they wanted to ensure their government-issued phones weren't monitored. As agreed, they would not call or receive calls at times they were working or on assignment. She would call Kirk that evening because he was still on vacation, and they would be in more comfortable surroundings while talking.

Nur left the office shortly after 5:00 p.m. and drove to her apartment, a small efficiency in a swanky area of northwest DC. As discussed, she called Kirk from the small yard outside her residence, upon seeing the number on caller ID, he walked out on his own balcony before answering the call.

"I've been missing you all day," Nur said.

"The same goes for me," he replied. "All day long I wanted to come by the office and just happen to see that you'd returned to work."

Although the two were well aware of the lack of security on a phone, she did state that for the next two days she would be doing farm work. Kirk knew that meant she would be going to Langley's CIA headquarters, ostensibly for training purposes.

"Honey, when I return to the office, I'm going to bring up the matter we discussed on our vacation," Nur stated.

"I'll obviously leave that situation up to you," Kirk replied, "but I'm not so sure that a move at this point wouldn't be potentially harmful to your career, and other areas," he replied. "Just please give it some serious thought, but the decision is yours."

Following their conversation, Kirk returned to the confines of his small but elegantly appointed apartment. He realized that despite most aspects of his work, there were certain areas that he found extremely troubling. Although the CIA had eliminated Warren B. Knicely, the killer of Kirk's father, he had a strong feeling that his father would not have approved. Nor would he have approved of the killing of David Franklin Lowe when the spy was released from incarceration in Colorado. From the hours of bedside talks he'd recently had with Nur on these same matters, he knew that she fully agreed with his feelings.

On the brighter side, Kirk found no lingering sentiments in the government approach to handling the terrorists in Paris or Tennessee.

In the final analysis, Kirk Alexander realized that the federal government was becoming the judge and jury, and Kirk, along with the "dirty squad," were the executioners.

Chapter 80

Nur had enjoyed the two days she'd spent in refresher training and was intrigued with the newfound knowledge of mixing three over–the-counter substances, putting them into an ice tray, and ultimately placing the ice cube into a beverage glass which, when consumed, created a fatal heart attack whose source could not be detected.

She had also given constant consideration to her plans of leaving the intelligence group where she was assigned. Nur had finally come to the conclusion that she wanted a life that for once would be unencumbered with death. She'd seen enough of death when Saddam Hussein had unleashed his poisonous gas on so many members of her family in Kurdistan. She'd participated in the "art" of extinction with the US government. As Nur had shared with Kirk, she was ready to create, not take life. Nur wanted to experience motherhood and had chosen Kirk Alexander as her partner.

On her return to work, Nur waited until Leonard Oathmeyer was alone and asked if he would allow her a few minutes to discuss a problem.

"Lennie, I just can't live this life any longer," Nur candidly stated. She was careful to avoid any mention of Kirk, yet she shared her fears from being kidnapped in Paris, her aversion to taking other people's lives into her own hands, and the desire to fully realize the American dream of finding Mr. Right and to cease being Ms. Wrong.

Leonard Oathmeyer listened attentively, nodded his head in tacit agreement, and hid behind a poker face that would have misled any Las Vegas gambler. "Nur, have you discussed your thoughts and plans with anyone else?" he finally asked.

"No," she lied. "You're the only person I would share it with."

Leonard Oathmeyer thought contemplatively and then smiled broadly.

"I have a couple of positions I may be able to assign to you, but it would take a couple of weeks to set up," he stated. "While I'm doing my due diligence here, I want you to handle a routine surveillance in Miami. This will take you completely away from violence but also give you something to work on in the meantime."

Nur Jasim felt so relieved. Her instincts had been right when making her decision that Lennie would be understanding and fair, as he had always demonstrated.

"Prepare a few identities for Miami, and I'll put your assignment together," Lennie said. "Also, I caution you not to discuss our conversation with anyone. I don't want any other employees to see there's a soft side to me."

Nur could not have been happier. More than ever she realized that her adopted country was the greatest country in the world, and she was surrounded by the greatest natural resources any country could have—great people.

She returned to her desk and began preparing cover identities for her trip to the sunny shores of Miami, Florida.

Chapter 81

The moment that Nur Jasim walked from his office, Leonard Oathmeyer began to put her assignment together.

An intelligence report from Homeland Security had identified a Cuban national as a person of interest who was possibly involved in bringing illegal aliens into the United States through the use of "mother ships," which would anchor outside US waters and turn their human cargo over to smaller speedboats.

As Lennie reviewed the file, he realized that the target, Javier LaCuna, was considered a ladies' man, and Nur would be an excellent choice to infiltrate his life and ongoing operations. The most important factor that Oathmeyer considered was that LaCuna wasn't being targeted for death. The intelligence team wanted enough evidence on his operations that would lead to cultivating him as an informant for the government.

Lennie carefully copied contents of the file and took them to Nur.

"This one should not only be fun, but it won't have the element of danger that you're used to facing," he stated. "By the time you wrap this up, your next assignment will be more rewarding."

Upon returning to his office, Lennie closed his soundproof door and called Kirk Alexander's number.

"Sorry to cut your vacation short," he told Kirk, "but I need to see you in my office tonight at 7:00."

"I'll be there," Kirk replied.

Chapter 82

Kirk had wondered throughout the afternoon what was as important as a night meeting with Lennie. He finally decided that it was impossible to figure out the impossible; he would find out soon enough when he met with his boss.

Kirk had not been able to contact Nur because he knew she was working. The two had decided that they should confine their contact to later at night, and so he decided he would wait until his 7:00 p.m. meeting was finished before making contact.

When he arrived for his scheduled appointment, Alexander knew immediately, from the expression on Lennie's face, that there were problems.

"This is the most serious problem I've encountered in my thirty-five years of government service," Lennie began.

Kirk noted that a large manila folder was open on the desk in front of Lennie.

"Several months ago, after Nur Jasmin was kidnapped, I provided an opportunity for her to have facial reconstruction to ensure her position here wasn't compromised," Lennie stated. "While she was in a private facility in Rhode Island, we know that Nur received three visits from an individual, an Iranian, whom we identified as being at the forefront of terrorist activities in the New York area. In short, Nur, in whom we gave our complete trust, has become a mole for the Iranians and now places our entire operation in jeopardy.

"Kirk, I now have Nur scheduled for a short operation in Miami," Lennie continued. "It's going to be up to you to protect the government by ensuring that Nur is terminated through some type of accident before she can do further harm to our government, our agency, and our own lives."

Kirk could not believe what he was hearing. He could only guess that Nur had followed up on their own conversations by talking to Lennie about leaving the intelligence field.

For added emphasis, Leonard Oathmeyer threw a grainy photograph on the table that showed an older man sitting with Nur in a garden setting.

"Is this the Iranian?" Kirk asked.

"That's the SOB who wants to destroy our country," Lennie replied.

Kirk realized that he was looking at a photograph of himself, in complete disguise, when he'd visited Nur in Rhode Island on one of several occasions. Kirk knew that Oathmeyer had no idea at all that he may be closer to Nur than any other employee in the government. He also realized that for Nur to remain alive, it was up to himself to come up with the perfect plan.

"When do you want me to leave for Florida, boss?" Kirk asked.

"Our spy is leaving tomorrow," Lennie replied. "I want you to give her a couple of days to become involved in her assignment. Maybe you can arrange an accident for both her and her target. It will get rid of two problems who threaten this great nation."

Kirk was sick to his stomach when leaving the director's entrance to the Bureau of Prisons. He had seen Leonard Oathmeyer not only walk on the Constitution of the United States of America, but also dance on it as if he were on *Dancing with the Stars.*

Before he left the parking lot of BOP, Kirk retrieved his prepaid cellular from the glove box of his car and dialed Nur's number with the speed dial. She answered on the second ring.

"Don't talk, but listen closely," Kirk said. "Do you remember the spot that you mentioned while in New York as being the most romantic location in the city of Washington?" Kirk asked.

"How could I ever forget?" was the immediate reply.

"Meet me there immediately, and make sure you're not followed," Kirk added.

"Okay," she said.

"One other thing," Kirk stated. "Kill anyone who approaches you unless it's me." He terminated the call.

Kirk drove aimlessly for a full twenty minutes before heading toward his destination. He was totally secure in the fact that he wasn't being followed before parking his car a block from the Potomac River. He'd decided that he would jog the remainder of the way, an opportunity to clear his own mind, with the added security of spotting anyone who might tail him.

From their previous conversation when Nur had mentioned the most romantic spot she knew in Washington, Kirk knew that she always jogged to this location. He began running in the direction from where she would come and, after a short while, ran off the path into a small wooded area where he would have a clear field of view.

After five minutes of observation, Kirk saw Nur as she jogged along the cement walkway along the Potomac River. As she passed, scarcely fifty yards away, his vantage point ensured she wasn't being followed. He waited a full three minutes before leaving his own position and heading back toward the direction she'd been heading.

As Kirk approached the spot, he looked out over the river and fully realized why she felt this way. The view of Reagan International Airport that was directly across the river was captivating.

Unfortunately, this was not the time to enjoy captivating views.

An hour before, Nur Jasmin was the only target on the horizon. Now, the two were partners in the same foxhole and facing a most competent enemy.

The two held each other closely for a full five minutes before retreating to a more secluded area where they began exchanging information about the recent turn of events.

"Kirk, the only way you can stay alive is to come to Florida and leave me dead," Nur candidly stated. "I love you and can't ruin your life."

"That's not an option," Kirk stated. This line of reasoning had already flashed through Kirk's mind, but it wasn't the future he hoped to have.

Nur smiled knowingly at the candor of his dismissing her line of thought. The two discussed their predicament for several hours before agreeing on the only option that would provide at least a slight possibility of remaining alive. Nur would depart for Florida the following day as scheduled. Kirk would follow a couple of days later, ostensibly to terminate her life.

The two exchanged their vows of love before jogging off in different directions in their quest toward their destiny.

Chapter 83

Kirk arrived at the office early, and Lois Harding informed him that Lennie was on the way to attend the Senate confirmation hearings for Polly Ann Gregory. "Ms. Gregory should be the new secretary of interior before the day is out," she stated.

Kirk immediately went to his own desk and began researching phone directories. Within an hour he'd produced enough passports, driver's licenses, credit cards, and ID cards to last indefinitely. Additionally, Kirk issued identification cards for most federal agencies, including the Federal Bureau of Investigation.

While Kirk worked, he occasionally referred to a small, handwritten list of the chores he needed to perform.

When Lois Harding left to pick up breakfast in the BOP cafeteria, Kirk immediately accessed other areas of the office and the communications network, for equipment and data that may be useful in the future.

As he performed his due diligence, Kirk smiled and realized that during his period of employment with the Bureau of Prisons, he'd developed a routine where he could create himself another identify within minutes.

By noon, Kirk had filled a briefcase with the documents he would need in the near and hopefully distant future. While Lois was away from the office, he accessed Nur's desk with the combination she'd provided and removed and copied file records that dated back to her first and subsequent assignments completed during her tenure with the US government. The file was thick!

Before leaving the office for his assignment in Miami, a jubilant Lennie Oathmeyer came into the office and excitedly announced to Kirk and Lois that Polly Ann Gregory had just been confirmed as the fiftieth secretary of interior. He also informed the two that Greg Wilson had accepted the position as director of the Bureau of Prisons.

"We only have a few loose ends to tie up," Lennie stated while looking into Kirk Alexander's eyes.

Kirk was well aware of the loose ends to which he was referring.

"I'll take care of it, boss," he stated while walking out the office door with the fruits of the day's accomplishments.

Chapter 84

Kirk realized he had a lot of work to complete in a short time. He drove to the Watergate and, after checking mail, proceeded to his apartment.

His flight was scheduled to depart Dulles International Airport at 2:45 p.m. the following day, and Kirk wanted to get as much accomplished in the remaining time as he could. He didn't discount the fact that upon arrival in Miami, he would have a fair degree of latitude before having to produce for Lennie.

Alexander walked to his balcony and made a quick call to Nur, who said she had safely made the trip to Florida, was registered in her hotel, and would be spending most of the next day doing research on Javier LaCuna.

"Just don't underestimate the potential of anything unusual," Kirk cautioned.

Nur realized that he was referring to the possibility that others, besides Kirk, may have received their own assignment of assassinating her.

The two agreed they would meet the following evening at a small Cuban restaurant that Nur had discovered in the area of her hotel.

"I'll watch the farm from this end," Nur stated, with an obvious reference to directives that could potentially have been given by certain powers at Langley.

When reviewing the details obtained from the most sensitive files maintained at the Bureau of Prisons, Kirk realized just how active Nur had been in her employment with the government. Lennie Oathmeyer, it appeared, had attempted to program Nur as a killing machine, which left Kirk wondering how she had managed to maintain any moral standards at all.

He finally resolved that her love for the United States was such that she wouldn't question any orders received from superiors. Although Kirk also loved his country, he realized that his employment with the government was more conditional in that if his father's killer, Warren Knicely, had not been terminated, Kirk Alexander probably wouldn't have accepted the employment offer.

For the next three hours, Kirk researched both his and Nur's personal data information and wrote copious notes providing the who, what, when, where, why, and how of every assignment the two had jointly or individually been assigned.

"If my country is going to kill me and the one I love," Kirk thought, "then they're going to have a dose of senatorial revenge," he reasoned.

Sleep was slow and troubling to find as Kirk Alexander tossed and turned throughout the long night.

The following morning he was awake early and worked feverishly to complete the myriad tasks that waited.

Chapter 85

"Have a safe journey, Mr. Tennyson," said the transportation safety administration officer, and Kirk walked past the ticket gate and down the ramp leading to his flight.

Kirk had decided to fly under the name of Franklin S. Tennyson, a senior field supervisor for the Department of Homeland Security. Kirk knew that this identity would ensure he wasn't delayed with inspections of his personal effects The flight to Miami was smooth and uneventful, and Kirk sat in his business class seat while his mind worked overtime to resolve problems that were yet to be created.

Before his scheduled dinner with Nur, Kirk would be able to purchase some items that would be necessary in completing his plans, but at the same time he was fully cognizant that both he and Nur could become very dead at any moment.

Upon arrival at Miami International, he decided against renting a car and chose a taxi that was parked at the curb of the passenger arrival door. It dawned on Kirk that in his haste to deal with other issues, he had neglected to make hotel reservations. His driver was knowledgeable about the Miami Beach area and knew of a nice hotel just two blocks from the Havana Cabaña Restaurant, where Kirk would be meeting Nur.

As anticipated, the hotel did have a room available, and Franklin S. Tennyson was soon relaxing in a hot shower after, which he called Nur on his cellular phones and confirmed a time for dinner.

Kirk still had some shopping to do at the expense of the US Department of the Treasury.

To be on top of things, Kirk also called Lennie Oathmeyer on his government-issued cellular and advised he was on the ground in Miami.

"Stay safe and make it painless," Lennie almost jokingly stated before the call was ended.

Kirk seethed at the callousness that was exhibited by his employer. "Painless is not a word you're going to be exposed to," he thought as he connected his phone to a charger.

He wouldn't take his government cell phone with him when he went out because he knew the phone had global positioning capability that would keep his superiors informed of his location at all times. Kirk had shared this thought with Nur, who would also leave her phone at her hotel room when having any type of contact with her lover.

"Why would I want the phone?" Nur had asked. "Knowing Lennie, if I dialed 911, the call would probably be put on hold."

After observing the area of the restaurant for a full ten minutes, Kirk entered at exactly 7:30 p.m. and observed Nur seated in the rear of the restaurant, adjacent to an emergency fire exit.

When he approached the table, Kirk fought the impulse to kiss her, opting instead to squeeze her outstretched hand tightly. Although the two felt they were not under any type of surveillance, both knew that agents in their profession who didn't practice security didn't live too long.

Kirk brought Nur up to speed on his own plans and activities. She nodded her head in concurrence as he shared his ideas that could conceivably keep the couple alive for the long term, as long as they could manage an escape in the short term.

"Lennie proposed that I stage an accident that would take the lives of both you and your smuggler, Javier LaCuna," Kirk stated.

"I briefly met Javier at lunch today," she replied. "He suggested that because I'm vacationing here in Miami, perhaps I'd join him for a drink."

As the two discussed their predicament, an idea began to form in Kirk Alexander's mind. He would wait until a more opportune time to present his thoughts.

Despite the intense stress the agents were under, they enjoyed their meal and decided to return to Kirk's hotel to put their plan in action.

"I hope those are gifts for me," Nur said, referring to two shopping bags that Kirk had brought into the restaurant.

"Actually, I didn't have time to take them back to the hotel, and so I guess we'll just have to sit on our luggage" Kirk joked.

After finishing an excellent Cuban dinner, they agreed to meet at Kirk's hotel room in an hour. This would ensure the two weren't observed outside the restaurant together, and it would provide each of the agents an opportunity to confirm that they were not under any type of surveillance.

Kirk arrived at his hotel first and quickly opened the contents of his parcels. Thanks to the US government, Kirk had purchased a laptop computer that would replace the one issued by the government. He also opened a box that contained a video camcorder, which he quickly made ready for use.

Within minutes, Nur knocked lightly on the door, and after a quick glance through the peephole, Kirk opened the door and she entered. This time there was no handshake—just a long, wet kiss and a hug that lasted for several minutes.

"Are you sure you want to get involved in my mistake?" Nur asked.

"We both made huge mistakes in our choice of employment," he replied. "Let's see how long we can last in being a team outside the control of Lennie Oathmeyer."

It took Nur Jasmin over an hour to review her activity reports and prepare a video script that would be directed to Senator Royal T. Wingate. Nur spoke of her recruitment by the Central Intelligence Agency, assignment as an intelligence analyst for the Bureau of Prisons, and a concise detail of every assignment she'd received from Lennie Oathmeyer that also included dates, locations, and explicit details of her training.

Kirk had suggested that the video should give the senator enough room to claim deniability of knowledge, without flexibility of feigning complete lack of knowledge.

Kirk then inserted a fresh video into the camcorder and gave a synopsis of his own recruitment, training, assignments, and details of the clandestine operations.

"Senator Wingate, what you knew or when you knew it is not of interest to me," Kirk stated. "I do believe the American people will support the efforts of the CIA in the fight against terrorism, as I do, but don't believe they will interpret the killing of released prisoners as an act that is allowed under the Constitution of the United States of America."

Alexander ended his lengthy video by saying, "Either Leonard Oathmeyer worked alone in this ongoing process of murder or in concert with you, Senator Wingate. What happens to Lennie Oathmeyer, and what happens to Nur Jasim and me, will determine whether copies of our videos are released into the hands of the *New York Times* and *Washington Post*. One issue is clear: If Leonard Oathmeyer remains at his post, then accept the fact that through our own resources we will provide the American public with exceptional insight on the fight against terrorism—even if our voices speak from our graves."

Both Nur and Kirk felt drained following the preparation of the video, but they also felt a certain degree of exhilaration after having gotten so many dark secrets off their chest.

"Do you think we have a chance?" Nur asked.

"I was taught in a survival class that remaining alive is 90 percent skill and 10 percent luck," Kirk replied. "In our case, it will be 90 percent luck and 10 percent skill."

The two decided that Lennie Oathmeyer would not expect immediate results on behalf of either of his targeted operatives. Nur would need the time to gain the confidence of Javier LaCuna, and Kirk would need to find the opportunity to stage an accident when Nur and Javier were together.

The operatives decided they would not meet each other again while in Miami because the risks were too great. They would continue to converse through their personal cell phones and would meet only if an escape attempt was eminent.

Kirk then opened his briefcase and gave ten manila envelopes to Nur. Each contained passports in various names, accompanying driver licenses, and enough credit cards to last for an indefinite period of time.

"All of the identification was obtained through the Department of Justice database from the Witness Protection Program," Kirk said. "Lennie won't find anything amiss from our own office protocol."

It was shortly after 4:00 a.m., and the two decided it would be safer for Nur to leave Kirk's hotel under the added security of darkness.

Their kiss was long and tender as Nur turned to open the door to leave. When she walked into the hallway, her smile turned to wide-eyed shock that bordered on panic. Standing in the hallway, holding a gun that was pointed at Nur's heart, was Leslie "The Broom" McCarter.

Chapter 86

The Broom had made one jerk with the gun that convinced Nur she had to back into the room where Kirk stood.

"I suggest you both interlock your fingers on top of your heads," McCarter stated. "I don't believe I need to convince either of you of my proficiency with this particular weapon, and won't hesitate killing both of you now."

The Broom was holding one of the Glock 9mm pistols with noise suppression. Kirk and Nur were only too aware that when faced with an adversary as proficient as McCarter, one followed their directions explicitly or died on the spot.

"You are both aware of the reason that Lennie Oathmeyer sent me here," Leslie said. "As long as the two of you remained apart, then my assignment was to watch and verify that Kirk had fulfilled his assignment, by killing Nur. There are some issues involved in this particular assignment that present a dilemma. First, let me tell you both what I know, and perhaps either or both of you will shed some clarity on my confusion.

"In briefing me for this assignment, Lennie showed me a couple of photographs, ostensibly of an Iranian who visited Nur while she was in Rhode Island for surgery. The problem with the photograph was that I recognized Kirk as that alleged Iranian terrorist. Although Lennie didn't see it, I immediately recognized that the left foot turned in to the right while the left hand rested on top of the left knee—a physical characteristic I'd observed in Kirk on numerous occasions," McCarter said. "I need to determine why Lennie lied to me, at your expense, Nur.

"Second, both of your actions in Paris saved me from being taken out by a terrorist," he added. "I'm just an old soldier who will live for or die for my soldiers in combat. In short, it's hard for me to kill two soldiers who are solely responsible for me being alive today. I'm ready for either or both of you to make your case for staying alive."

Nur and Kirk looked at each other. In view of the fact that Leslie was primarily an outside contractor, could there be some elements of the office activities of which he wasn't aware?

"Leslie, will you watch a video that we prepared for Senator Wingate? If you watch the video and still believe we deserve to die, then either way you'll know the full story," Kirk volunteered.

Although he continued to hold the pointed weapon, McCarter nodded his head in agreement to watching the video, which Kirk inserted into the television. The group watched both videos in their entirety.

"So your only crime, Nur, was a desire to leave the CIA?" Leslie asked.

"That, and falling in love with a fellow agent," Nur replied while looking at Kirk.

"I provided backup to the both of you on a couple of your hits," McCarter stated. "But Lennie never told me the real reasons the hits were ordered. I would have blown the whistle years ago if I was aware of all of this. How were you going to get these videos to Senator Wingate?"

"We were still working on that angle," Kirk replied. "We knew that once Lennie was aware that I hadn't completed the killing of Nur, then we both would have been targeted. And, we aren't sure whether or not Senator Wingate has complete knowledge of what our staff is involved in."

"I know Senator Wingate very well," Leslie commented, "and I'd stake my life that he only knows of the necessary kills, not those arbitrary ones that Lennie may have ordered." He thought quietly for a full minute before speaking again. "Let's make a copy of your videos for me to take to Senator Wingate. Keep a copy for yourselves in the event I'm wrong, which will also mean Lennie will be dispatching some young, trigger-happy agent to terminate us all. You two should leave the country immediately, and if you determine that Leonard Oathmeyer has been killed, or has expired as a result of a heart attack, then the coast will be clear for you to return home. If you hear that I've died, then you'll know the senator was also in the wrong and knew about Lennie's actions."

A half hour later, Leslie McCarter had copies of the videos he would take to Senator Royal T. Wingate and promised that he would be on the first flight to Washington DC.

"Don't give me any details of your escape plans," Leslie cautioned. "If you don't hear anything from me or about the death of Lennie Oathmeyer, then you will know that I've found out you both were wrong, and I'll eventually find you. For now, you continue living because you saved my life in Paris."

McCarter quietly walked from the hotel room and into the night.

Chapter 87

Nur and Kirk had thought they were exhausted when Nur decided to leave the room to return to her own hotel. Following the departure of McCarter, the two were still exhausted yet wide awake. They needed to get out of the United States while their fate rested in the hands of Senator Wingate.

The two decided to remain in Kirk's room for a few hours of rest. Then they would formulate their plans on leaving the country.

"If we happen to live," Kirk stated, "I would like to someday find out how The Broom located us so quickly."

The couple slept soundly for five hours, tightly entwined in each other's arms. When they woke up. the beautiful sunlit sky made them both thankful they had survived the previous evening.

They discussed their plight for a couple of hours and gave birth to a plan that could conceivably get them out of the country. The pair decided that Nur would go to her hotel, get cleaned up, and make a couple of necessary phone calls. She would then contact Kirk with the results of her activities.

Kirk also cleaned up following Nur's departure, got dressed, and began watching CNN while waiting to hear from the woman he loved.

Chapter 88

Kirk had fallen asleep during the continuous newscast and was awakened by the ringing of his personal cellular phone. The call was from Nur, who asked, "Can we meet at 9:30 p.m. at the Royal Tropicana Bar on Ocean Boulevard?"

"I'll be there," Kirk replied. "Were you able to get the package?"

"I'm hopeful," she responded before hanging up.

At 9:15 p.m. a cab dropped Kirk off at the front entrance to the Royal Tropicana, an exclusive club in the middle of South Beach. Kirk was glad that he'd stopped at a local store and bought some clothing that would help him blend into the South Beach night life.

Carefully concealed in an ankle holster on his right leg was a weapon that would not be detected by a metal detector. Fortunately there were no such devices at this popular night spot.

Kirk sat at the bar carefully nursing a Jim Beam on the rocks when Nur walked through the front door. She was absolutely breathtaking in a sheer turquoise silk dress. Kirk felt a slight pang of jealousy as he noted that Nur was accompanying a male, obviously a man of means, who was drawing a considerable amount of attention as the two were quickly led to a small table in the club.

Kirk was aware that Nur had observed him when entering the club and waited for her nod before approaching the table. The two sat talking for several minutes, and Kirk noted that the gentleman with Nur glanced in his direction a couple of times.

Nur then nodded her head, and Kirk left the bar and walked to the table.

"Javier LaCuna, may I introduce you to my coworker and lover, Kirk Alexander."

LaCuna stood and warmly shook Kirk's hand before inviting him to join the couple.

"Javier, although I shared a little information with you, I believe that Kirk is prepared to make an offer to you that most prudent businessmen would gladly accept," Nur stated.

"Well, Kirk, what brings you to the beautiful sun and sand of Miami Beach?" Javier asked.

Kirk also possessed the ability to be charming and smiled broadly at Javier before beginning. "Quite frankly, Javier, I was sent here to set up a tragic accident in which you and Nur would perish together." Kirk then pulled a file from inside his silk shirt and carefully opened it. "This is a dossier that the US Government has put together, and which involves several of your 'business' enterprises." He then placed several surveillance photographs of LaCuna that had surreptitiously been obtained through covert surveillance of the smuggler.

The eyes of Javier LaCuna were wide as he looked at the still photographs and recalled the times when he would have been under surveillance.

"The fact is that Nur's life means significantly more to me that your own," Kirk stated. "I felt this entire folder—which, incidentally, gives the names of some of the informants being used to catch you—may be worth a trade."

Javier again looked at the file that was in front of Kirk. He knew this was not some crazed individual, but someone who had information that Lacuna's future successes depended on. "Mr. Kirk, you have already put your money where your mouth is. What would you be asking in return?" he questioned.

"Nur and I are going to run from our government, but we need a safe and secure way to leave the country," Kirk stated. "Javier, if you have the ability to bring illegal residents into this country by clandestine means, then I must assume you have the ability to get two legal citizens out of this country through those same clandestine means."

"What if I elected to kill you?" Javier asked.

"In that event," Kirk replied, "The government would assume that I failed in my assignment, and since you were the last assignment I was given, then you would be required to pay the penalty. Please remember that the same telephoto lens that attaches to cameras can be exchanged for a sniper scope that fits on the rifles of certain American employees. In short, Javier, what I give to you will keep you out of jail and out of a dirty old grave—at least for the foreseeable future. In return, you will discreetly, quietly, and quickly get Nur and me out of the United States."

"When would I receive the folder you possess?" Javier asked.

"I will give you the folder now," Kirk stated. "At the time that Nur and I safely land on foreign soil, I'll give you, or the person you delegate, a computer disk that has the names of every informant the US government is using to gain evidence against you."

Javier thought for several minutes before speaking. "Mr. Kirk, at 2:00 a.m., four hours from now, you both should be at the Miami Glades Marina in North Miami Beach. I will meet you personally and ride with you to a mother ship that will take you to Brazil. Is there anything else?"

"Only that it may be dangerous to us both if you inform your close associate, Jose Sanchez, of this discussion or our plans," Kirk cautioned.

Although Sanchez was not a government informant, Kirk realized he was taking an opportunity to ensure another adversary would be eliminated.   Kirk and Nur shook hands with their new associate and walked from the bar.

Before taking their packed bags to the Miami Glades Marina, they would have their taxi driver stop at a small bridge that crossed over the Intercoastal Waterway, at which point each of them would throw their government-issued cellular phones into the swift current.

As it turned out, the mother ship happened to be the private yacht of Javier LaCuna, a 120-foot luxury vessel that was registered in Sao Paulo, Brazil.

Chapter 89

Nur Jasim and Kirk Alexander were on their fourth day at sea with the expectation of hitting land near Sao Paulo sometime during the early morning hours. They had quickly determined that the ship's crew was professional and capable—and probably beneath their smooth demeanor, they could be extremely dangerous.

The two were lying in the master suite of the vessel watching the television when a significant news flash from Capitol Hill was reported.

During the previous night, Leonard Oathmeyer, a trusted aide and confidante to Senator Royal T. Wingate, had died in his sleep from a massive heart attack. The news release reported that a distraught Senator Wingate had stated that his friend Lennie was a true American who earned the respect of all levels of government in leading the fight against crime, corruption, and terrorism.

The concluding report gave Kirk and Nur the true answer they sought.

Senator Royal Wingate had named retired Army Sergeant Leslie McCarter as the operations director who would replace Leonard Oathmeyer on his staff.

"Does this mean we're going home?" Nur asked.

"Not until after the wedding," replied Kirk as he placed Big Bertha, the diamond from the Bureau of Prisons, on the ring finger of her left hand.

"I accept this ring with the full understanding that when we return to the states, it needs to be returned to the rightful owner, whoever the rightful owner is," Nur stated with a smile. Then she joked, "Perhaps something that is a bit more discreet would be fitting to our lifestyles and would keep photographs of my left hand off *America's Most Wanted*."

The two were in the process of completing their packing when the telephone inside the state room began ringing. The sound startled both Kirk and Nur because they had not previously heard it ring during their travel to freedom.

"Hello," Kirk stated when he picked up the receiver.

"Good evening, my friend," stated Javier LaCuna. "Are you two ready to travel to shore?" he asked.

"Whenever you give the word," Kirk replied.

"In one hour you need to meet a small craft that will take you ashore," Javier said. "There is only the matter of some information you're going to pass on to my captain before you leave on the continuation of your journey."

"I have it in my hand and will give it to the captain before leaving your craft," Kirk replied.

"With that, I wish you complete success in avoiding those who may want to delay or terminate your travels," replied Javier, and the phone disconnected.

Kirk quickly briefed Nur and retrieved a small memory stick for a computer from his pocket and laid it on the bed.

Nur quickly hugged and smiled at Kirk as they continued packing their belonging in a small back pack. "It's going to be so nice to purchase clothing when we get ashore," Nur remarked.

Kirk separated their false passports, credit cards, and cash from the rest of their luggage and placed them in a fanny pack, which he adjusted to secure it under his shirt.

"Perhaps it would be safer if you carry Big Bertha," Nur stated as she removed the diamond ring from her hand.

Kirk smiled knowingly as he zipped the ring inside his pack. They held hands and watched CNN while waiting for their departure.

Chapter 90

Nur and Kirk only had to wait a short time before a voice came over the ship's intercom advising them to come forward with their belongings.

"Ready for a new life?" Kirk asked.

"More ready than you'll ever realize," Nur's responded.

Kirk inserted a 9mm Glock into his ankle holster. "I'll drop it in the water when we get to shore," Kirk stated.

They proceeded out the door of their stateroom and walked to the forward deck, where the captain was waiting beside an open gate that revealed a small ladder leading down to a small speed boat that quietly bobbled on the light waves and had one occupant.

Kirk handed the computer memory stick to the captain, who smiled. "Have a safe journey, my friend," stated the captain as the two quickly left the mother ship and climbed down to the smaller craft.

The lone pilot of the small craft nodded his head at the his passengers as they sat down in the front of the boat and looked toward the glittering lights of Porto Seguro, Brazil, a mere two miles away. The Donzi speedboat skimmed along the water toward the inviting lights of the city as Kirk looked back and realized that all lighting from their previous vessel had been extinguished; only a shadow moved along the water from the area they had just left. Kirk imagined that LaCuna's ship would travel several miles under blackout conditions until the captain felt safe in the international waters outside the coastal area of Brazil.

As the Donzi approached a darkened area of land, just east of the city, Kirk noted a flashlight turning on and off twice, an obvious indication to the captain of the Donzi of the course he needed to maintain to drop off the passengers.

Both Kirk and Nur breathed a sigh of relief with the realization that they were so close to melting into a dark cloak of anonymity.

As the craft got closer to land, the pilot slowed the speedboat back to idle as the powerful boat slowly approached the shoreline. Kirk could see a shadowy figure waiting beside a small boathouse, scarcely thirty yards away.

A slight splash at the rear of the Donzi caused Kirk to look toward the rear, and he immediately realized the captain had gone into the water. Kirk turned to Nur to yell a warning. As he looked at the face of his lover, her beautiful features exploded, showering the interior of the boat with brains, blood, and portions of her skull as the bullet exited the back of her head. Kirk realized that the assailant was using a rifle that was equipped with a silencer—and he also knew that he was the next target.

Kirk quickly assessed the situation and determined that his only chance for survival was to get away from the boat, which continued on its path to the shoreline. He dove over the side of the boat, feeling the rush of air of a bullet that passed where his own head had just been.

Kirk thought that the captain of the small speedboat would have logically been the first target. While in the water he could see the figure of the pilot of the boat swimming toward shore, a mere twelve yards away. The fact that the captain was swimming toward shore proved to Kirk the complicity between the killer on land and the figure in the water. The young agent silently dove toward the shallow bottom and, with the stealth of an attacking shark, swam along the bottom toward the fleeing captain, who never had the opportunity to sense danger until the moment he was suddenly pulled under the water and died from a very broken neck.

Kirk surfaced and assumed the place of the boat captain as he silently swam toward shore.

"Luco?" whispered a voice from the shoreline as Kirk approached.

"Si," Kirk's responded as the figure walked toward the shoreline to assist the person he thought was his cohort from the black water. As a helping hand was extended to Kirk, Nur's killer suddenly realized he had been less than successful in killing both of his targets. The killer was immediately pulled headfirst into the water where he was viciously strangled to death at the water's edge.

Kirk sat momentarily as he considered his plight. He was in a secluded area, perhaps a half mile from the town of Porto Seguro. The Donzi was resting on the shore with the powerful engine continuing to run, and the bodies of two killers were within several yards of his location.

He noticed the body of the speedboat pilot floating silently a few yards away. Kirk waded out, retrieved the remains, and brought them to shore where he roughly laid the body next to that of the dead killer, whose rifle still hung around his neck.

He then walked to the Donzi, reached inside, and gently lifted the body of Nur from her death bed and placed her remains on the shore. He retrieved the bodies of their assailants from the shoreline and dumped them into the passenger area of the speedboat.

Kirk was an individual who had received extensive training and preparation in the concept of situational awareness, and he quickly formulated a plan to discard the bodies of the assailants while ensuring that Nur's remains would be preserved for return to the United States.

A quick assessment of the equipment and supplies on board the Donzi revealed a rod and reel that contained heavy monofilament fishing line. Kirk backed the Donzi off the shore and turned the boat around to a position where it faced the open water. He then removed the belts from the waist of his assailants and used one to secure the boat's steering mechanism, which would ensure it would proceed straight toward the open water. Kirk took the rifle that had been used to kill Nur and which had been almost successful in taking his own life. He ensured a live bullet was in the chamber of the rifle and ready to fire. He then affixed the hook that was attached to the monofilament line to the trigger of the rifle and carefully laid the rifle on the deck of the boat before laying the fishing rod onto the shoreline. Kirk located a small gas can that contained approximately two gallons of gasoline and poured the contents on the floor of the Donzi.

The young intelligence operative then checked to be sure that the boat was in neutral and took the second assailant's belt to secure the boat's accelerator lever, ensuring the boat would maintain a continual slow speed in its journey.

Kirk inspected his rigging and was satisfied with the results. He then straddled the side of the boat, reached over and pushed the forward lever, and jumped off the boat as it began its journey toward the open water.

Kirk was back at the fishing rod before the boat had traveled a significant distance. He held the rod in his hand as the reel fed monofilament line to the departing boat. Kirk sat next to the lifeless body of the woman he loved as he listened to the Donzi as it departed, only connected to the world by a monofilament umbilical cord that he held in his hand.

When the boat was far enough from land to be in deep water, he closed the housing of the reel, which immediately quit feeding line to the slowly moving boat. The fishhook held onto the trigger as the hammer of the rifle was pulled. It sent a muzzle blast that immediately caused the gasoline to explode. The silenced rifle had not made a sound, the Donzi was out of hearing range, and Kirk suddenly witnessed a beautiful pyrotechnic display in the distance. He knew there was no time to waste and felt secure that the Donzi would burn its passengers' bodies and sink within minutes. Kirk had not left a crime scene for the authorities to investigate.

Kirk Alexander reached under his shirt and retrieved his small fanny pack. He quickly went through the contents and removed an American passport that displayed Nur's picture, which identified her as Jennifer Marie Parton. Kirk placed the passport in the pocket of the light jacket Nur was wearing, patted her shoulder, and said: "I love you and will think of you every day for the rest of my life."

He then began hastily walking toward the city lights of the small village while removing a small cellular phone from a plastic bag inside his backpack.

Chapter 91

Leslie McCarter was not surprised to hear from his messenger, but he completely floored when he received the report. He knew that Kirk was calling from a phone that wasn't secure; therefore the conversation was brief.

The Broom advised his operative to return to Washington, and they would prepare a dish called revenge for the mastermind who remained somewhere in Florida. Kirk provided Nur's cover identity, which The Broom could use in tracking the remains of his deceased agent.

McCarter would have the US State Department assist in locating one of their citizens, a missionary named Jennifer Marie Parton, and return her remains to the United States, where she could receive a proper burial. As anticipated, authorities in the small fishing village of Porto Seguro would only be able to provide a short narrative relating to their investigation. "Ms. Parton was shot to death by an unknown person about the same time that a speedboat exploded offshore." Authorities did not have any grounds to associate the two occurrences, and no projectiles were recovered that could link to a ballistic comparison. In view of the fact that no money or credit cards had been found on the body, it was assumed by law enforcement that robbery was the motive for the crime, which may have occurred while she was fishing at the secluded area.

Kirk wasted no time in securing transportation to Sao Paulo, where he would discard his weapon and return to the relative safety of the city of Washington.

Chapter 92

Kirk had decided to travel from Sao Paulo to Dulles International Airport, in Washington DC, by using a diplomatic US passport in the name of Winston C. Fletcher. This selection of identity had proved to be beneficial in view of the fact that Brazilian authorities at the airport were unable to locate records of Mr. Fletcher entering the country, yet customs personnel were not about to interfere with the travel of a US State Department analyst who was traveling under a diplomatic passport. Mr. Fletcher was quickly issued a boarding pass and thanked for visiting the country.

Prior to arrival at the airport, Kirk had disposed of all passports and documents associated with Nur, disassembled the Glock, and discarded the pieces of the weapon in various locations where recovery would be highly unlikely.

As Kirk sat in the business class of the flight, he realized that he had been fortunate in life in the fact that he'd only lost three people he'd loved: his father, his mother, and now the woman he'd wanted as his lifelong mate, Nur.

As tears welled in his eyes, Kirk felt anger, and despite his ability to hurt, he didn't have the capacity to completely express the pain he was experiencing. The one consoling aspect in his heart was that he knew that Nur would understand his actions following her death and would have reacted and responded in the same manner.

There were other issues that needed to be addressed in Kirk's mind that he knew would assist in the healing process.

First, Javier LaCuna was the only person who knew where Kirk and

Nur would be at a specific time and place. There was absolutely no chance that anyone other than LaCuna had been the one who betrayed the two. There remained a small degree of fate involved in Javier's decision. When Kirk and Nur had reviewed the countless pages of intelligence on LaCuna's operations, they had ignored the names of personnel who were actually being used by the government to provide information on LaCuna. In fact, the memory stick that Kirk had provided to the captain of LaCuna's vessel contained the names of those who the government was sure would not provide information that would lead to his downfall. In short, and with a bit of luck, in a matter of days Javier LaCuna would be killing those who were most faithful to him and his smuggling empire.

Kirk felt confident that his first official assignment under the leadership of Leslie McCarter would be to dismantle the operation and, hopefully, the body of Javier LaCuna.

He would not be disappointed in his assumption.

Chapter 93

Leslie McCarter had used his clout as the director of Operations for Senator Royal T. Wingate in lighting a fire in the Office of Protocol at the US State Department. In fact, and completely unknown to Kirk, the remains of Nur Jasmin were in the cargo hold of the very plane on which he was a passenger.

The Broom had also reached out to his counterparts within the intelligence community, and information relating to the activities of Javier LaCuna was being forwarded to McCarter on a minute-to-minute basis.

Even Senator Wingate, whose previous operations director had placed a death edict on Nur Jasmin, was demanding retribution for her death. "Leslie, I will not allow injury to our operatives when they're trying to save what's left of our country," Wingate had stated on several occasions since learning of the death of Nur. "I'm leaving it up to you and your boys to clean up this mess."

The Broom had learned from a text message that Kirk would arrive from Brazil during the late evening and would be in the Bureau of Prison office the next morning.

McCarter accessed a website on his computer and determined that Kirk's flight was just off the coast of Miami and proceeding toward Dulles. He had not been advised by Kirk of his specific flight. There was no need to transmit specific information because Big Bertha, the ring, contained a global positioning transmitter under the massive diamond.

In fact, Leslie had monitored the travels of Nur and Kirk every minute since they had departed Miami aboard Javier LaCuna's ship. If Kirk had known this information, perhaps he would have also included the "dirty boys" as possible suspects in the untimely death of Nur Jasmin.

Chapter 94

Kirk felt clean for the first time in several days. Upon arrival at the Watergate apartments, he'd retrieved and reviewed his mail that had accumulated during the past few days and had poured himself a glass of Jim Beam before soaking in a hot tub for a full hour.

He actually felt like he'd been away from the office for an eternity and looked forward to the first day of work under the helm of Leslie McCarter. Although Kirk had enjoyed working for Lennie Oathmeyer, his personal observations of McCarter had reflected a man who distanced himself more from the political side of government service and was more in tune with the mission. In one of their previous conversations, Leslie had made a statement that had stuck with Kirk. "Personnel first, mission always."

The Broom was already at his desk when Kirk arrived. Lois was at the coffee pot to welcome him back with a quick hug and expression of sorrow on the loss of Nur.

Leslie McCarter wasted no time in bringing Kirk up to date on the recent turn of events. "I know you're aware that Lennie Oathmeyer succumbed to a massive heart attack a few days ago," he stated. "I've been designated to assume his role but have been given the mandate of having considerably more leeway than Lennie had. Our unit will no longer be involved with retribution toward any confined prisoners—unless, of course, they were directly involved in terrorist activities. The POTUS, through Senator Wingate, has delegated our small group of "dirty boys" as the lead unit for black operations involving terrorists. The only exception to our newly assigned mandate is that we remain the designated team to take out the LaCuna operation. That is because Nur Jasmin was one of ours, and we will not leave Nur's memory on a battlefield where there remains a need to fight. In short, You and I are going to deal with LaCuna."

Kirk smiled inwardly with the knowledge that he was being provided free rein on a mission that he'd sworn to himself would be completed.

"Senator Wingate also agrees with me that accepting employment with the CIA or Bureau of Prisons should not make us personal property of that agency," Leslie continued. "In short, our personnel can love who they love, hate those they hate, but can only kill with direction and permission. With that being said, let's start making our plans to repay Javier LaCuna for the anguish he's created in this world.

Kirk and McCarter worked for several hours as they reviewed both old and fresh information related to LaCuna. Wiretap information provided documentation that Javier had, in fact, given direction to have Kirk and Nur killed as they approached the shore in Brazil. More recent phone intercepts indicated that two of the names provided by Kirk on the memory stick had been targeted for death.

It was apparent that Javier LaCuna believed the information provided by Kirk to be accurate.

"A win for the good guys," Kirk noted.

"Tomorrow you'll report to the farm for some refresher training, and on Wednesday the two of us will be flying on a military flight to Miami to complete our mission," McCarter said.

For security reasons, McCarter advised Kirk that none of the personnel within the Bureau of Prisons system would be authorized to attend Nur's pending funeral. "We just can't allow the potential lapse of security. We'll pay our proper respects to Nur in Florida. I'll bring all the hardware we need to send Javier on his final voyage."

Kirk and McCarter agreed to meet in two days at Andrews Air Force Base in Maryland, where they would depart for their mission in Miami. The two concurred that they would have all credentials reflecting that they were detectives with the Miami police department.

Kirk went to his own desk and began preparing the police credentials and papers under the name of Jonathan L. Higgins. Before leaving the office, Kirk would provide his cover name to guarantee Leslie would obtain authorization for Jonathan Higgins to have access to the sprawling air base and flight line.

Chapter 95

The following day, Kirk could only wonder about the particular block of training he was receiving. He'd anticipated firearms, yet the entire day was spent in throwing well-balanced knives, surreptitious attacks while utilizing a knife, and stealth attacks that required him to carefully creep up on a target from the back, grabbing the victim from the rear, and maliciously cutting the throat of the target.

Kirk could only wonder what type of retaliation The Broom might be planning. The entire day of refresher training involved much more than the professional side of killing—it centered on the personal aspect of revenge.

At the end of the day, the instructor, Luis Caballo, a young, well-trained marine from Quantico, cleared the confusion of the day's training. "Sir, I was instructed to give these items to you upon completion of your display of competency," Caballo stated. He then handed a leather carrying bag to Kirk that contained the four precision knives he'd trained with throughout the day.

It was suddenly very clear to Kirk that his assignment, which would begin the following day, was programmed to be very deadly yet extremely personal.

Leslie McCarter sure knew the right therapy in assisting his personnel work through issues of personal rage. As Kirk held the leather knife container, it dawned on him just how personal his rage was.

Kirk gave his young instructor a high five as he turned and walked back to his vehicle. He slept better that evening than any night since boarding the ship with Nur.

Chapter 96

Kirk arrived at the designated hangar at Andrews Air Force Base a full hour before the scheduled departure. He had packed items that would blend into the cover of darkness, and his arsenal of knives was carefully packed in an outer pocket of his luggage. Alexander only had to wait a short time before he observed Leslie McCarter parking a dated pickup truck and approaching the terminal with a duffle bag.

Kirk met his boss in the parking lot, and they walked into the terminal together where Leslie identified the two at the flight operations desk. Within minutes, they were escorted toward a C-124 cargo plane, and they carried their baggage on board and took two seats in a secluded area.

"We're going to land at Homestead Air Force Base and will have transportation provided by the military to our hotel in Miami Beach," Leslie stated. "I decided that flying directly into Miami International may be a bit indiscreet, considering the mess we're about to leave on the streets of Miami."

Kirk nodded knowingly, and the conversation changed to other events of the day and some of the future plans Leslie had for members of his team. It was readily apparent that Leslie McCarter was a hands-on manager who wanted to join his team on any assignments in which he could be involved. McCarter was not Lennie Oathmeyer, a fact that was heartwarming to Kirk.

The flight to Homestead was uneventful, and as planned, a discreet Ford Crown Victoria was waiting on the tarmac when the two departed the plane. The driver was not one to invite conversation, and in approximately one hour, the passengers exited at the South Beach Plaza Hotel.

Although they were registered in separate rooms, Leslie instructed

Kirk to come to his own room in an hour. They would discuss their plans at that time. After relaxing and taking a quick shower, Kirk knocked on the door of McCarter's room and was quickly admitted.

Leslie had already taken the opportunity to check his e-mails and advised Kirk that the latest intelligence from Washington indicated that LaCuna was planning on meeting with two of his associates at his residence that evening. "LaCuna has been expressing concern that he's been unable to contact his employee in Porto Seguro," The Broom stated. "Our analyst is not convinced it's become a major issue, but his anxiety could make him a bit more cautious."

The two then secured the room and rode the elevator to the ground floor, where the hotel clerk had keys to a rental car that had been delivered.

After locating the vehicle, McCarter retrieved a small GPS device from his bag. He had previously programmed the home address of Javier LaCuna into the mechanism, and they were pleased to see they were only a mile from the mansion where LaCuna resided. For the next two hours the operatives conducted surveillance of the residence and the surrounding area. The beach front of the home would provide access to the property, which would preserve their energy because they would not have to climb the high barricade fences that were on the street side of the property.

There was even a small public park a block from the residence where their rental vehicle could be parked.

Leslie and Kirk then returned to their hotel and proceeded to McCarter's room, where Leslie removed papers from his attaché case.

"Here are the blueprints to LaCuna's home," Leslie said, "complete with the location of a hiding area that was added two months ago. We should anticipate that if he somehow disappears while in his home, he'll use this safe room as a safety zone.

"One advantage that we have is that there is a small brass lamp affixed to the right side of the door. Push the button on the light, and the door will slide open from the left side. Needless to say, this room is well fortified with Kevlar material, and we should anticipate that LaCuna will be well armed if he makes it to this room."

Kirk knew that the information McCarter was providing would be accurate but wondered what agency had the resources to obtain this valuable data.

The Broom then removed a Walther PPK automatic from his bag and handed it to Kirk along with three clips of ammunition. The weapon was equipped with a silencer.

"It's considerably quieter than even a silenced Glock," Leslie stated. "Not quite as much firepower, so aim for their heads to get best results. If at all possible, use the knives you brought with you. We need to ensure that silence is in fact golden."

The two sat for over an hour as they reviewed aerial photographs of LaCuna's home, blueprints of the residence, and area maps.

"We will plan on entering the home through the beach side of the residence at exactly 10:00 p.m. At 9:57 p.m., I will receive a text message that will tell us exactly where in the home any human may be located. Anyone who sees our faces, including service personnel, must not be left alive," Leslie somberly stated.

Kirk nodded in acceptance with his handler's instructions.

"There are a couple of other items I want to share with you," McCarter continued. "Whenever we're dealing with retribution, we have a tendency to overkill rather than just get the mission accomplished. Nothing we do tonight will bring Nur back to us. Therefore we only need to concentrate on the mission, our objectives, and escape."

Kirk completely understood the message McCarter was conveying. Although he wanted to punish LaCuna, intellectually Kirk recognized their mission was to quickly and efficiently remove a problem. Kirk would not allow personal feelings to interfere with the task at hand.

Chapter 97

At exactly 9:37 p.m., Leslie McCarter drove into the public park near Javier LaCuna's home and pulled his vehicle adjacent to other cars that had stopped to enjoy the sounds of the slight waves as they continuously landed on the sandy beach. Cloud coverings provided additional security for the two government agents as they again reviewed their pending assignment.

Neither heard the sound of the CIA surveillance plane as it approached the area and utilized infrared equipment to pinpoint the heat from human bodies that were inside the targeted residence.

As anticipated, at 9:57 p.m. McCarter received a text message that indicated there were four individuals inside the LaCuna estate. Three of the targets were inside a den that overlooked the ocean, and the fourth occupant was located in the kitchen on the south side of the home.

The two agents quickly exited their car and melted into the darkness as they walked along the beach toward the estate.

"The fact that they don't have security on the exterior of the home could prove to be a costly mistake for LaCuna," McCarter whispered.

Kirk nodded knowingly.

The two crept along the line of palm trees that separated the home from the wide expanse of beach. Bright interior lighting illuminated two glass patio doors that led from the home to a beautiful patio setting. Both operatives recognized that the lighting could also illuminate them once they got too close to the door.

McCarter motioned for Kirk to stop as he bent to the ground and crawled toward the doorway.

Leslie McCarter was nothing more than a brief shadow as he slowly raised his head, evaluated the situation, and then quickly crawled back to where Kirk stood in the shadows. "LaCuna and two others are sitting in the den, playing cards," he stated. "Check it out so you know the layout."

Kirk immediately squatted to the ground and crawled to the same surveillance site where McCarter had been. As Kirk quickly looked into the room, he could see the three sitting at a large poker table. The manner in which the card players were sitting would ensure the two agents would have at least a small element of surprise upon entering the home.

"We go to plan B," McCarter whispered as Kirk backed away from the door and joined his boss. Plan B was to enter the home through a ground floor downstairs window on the north side of the home. They had already discussed this option as affording them the opportunity to surreptitiously enter the home without being visible to the occupants.

At the side window, Kirk quickly removed a knife from its sheath and pried the window up. It was immediately apparent that the window was locked.

Without a moment's hesitation, McCarter applied duct tape to a small area of window glass nearest the lock, removed a glass cutter from his vest pocket, and cut in a circular motion. He then pulled the heavy industrial tape, and a small portion of the window that covered the lock was removed.

Kirk inserted his knife through the hole in the pane of glass, quietly pushed the tip of the blade against the lock, and soundlessly unlocked the lever. He once again placed his knife at the bottom of the window and pried up. There was scarcely a sound as the window rose.

Within moments, both assassins were inside the bedroom and began slowly creeping toward the closed door that separated the den from the small guest room where the two had made entry.

Leslie and Kirk made their way to the door and prepared themselves for the attack. They had previously agreed that Kirk would first target LaCuna if he had a clear shot. Kirk would be the first to go into the den but would enter in such a manner that McCarter's own access into the den would not be impeded.

Leslie quietly touched Kirk on his right shoulder, a silent message that he was ready when Kirk made his entry into the den. Kirk turned the door handle, and the two quickly entered the den where the three targets played cards and smoked their Cuban cigars.

LaCuna was the first to look at the intruders who had so quietly entered his domain. He displayed a look of surprise and then panic as he recognized Kirk, who was already in the process of throwing a knife. The blade entered Javier's chest with such velocity that it buried to the hilt.

Meanwhile, Leslie McCarter quickly fired the silenced PPK into the heads of the other two card players, who had only managed to make feeble attempts to pull their own weapons.

Kirk quickly ran over to LaCuna, whose eyes revealed he knew he was a dying man. Kirk hastily extracted his throwing knife from LaCuna's chest, pointed his own automatic pistol at the center of the dying man's forehead, and blew the contents of his brain throughout the den.

The two Americans hurriedly opened the door that led to the ocean and melted into the darkness and comfort of Miami Beach.

Within minutes they were on the way to their hotel, where they would spend the night and depart for Washington the following day.

"Son, I think we should meet at my room for a drink," The Broom stated. "After all, we're flying to Yemen on Thursday to convince some terrorist rag heads that sending explosives to our Jewish synagogues isn't kosher."

The End